WHEN SLEEPING DOGS LIE

Henrietta F. Ford

Henrietta F. Ford

Second Printing

Other Books by Henrietta F. Ford

Angels in the Snow
Murder on the OBX
The Hessian Link
The Grave House Guest

To my best friend, Jim.

Your help and encouragement made this book possible.

Characters

Noah Murray—Matt's mentally challenged cousin
Matt Murray—visitor to his former home
Benjamin Day—Matt's friend and travel companion
Ignatius Harder—Matt's friend and travel companion
Aunt Peedee Murray—Matt's eccentric Aunt
Margot Pellinger—Matt's cousin
Einer Pellinger—Margot's wealthy influential husband
Audrey Kelly—local Police Detective
Donald Anderson—local Police Detective
Steve Murray—Matt's older brother
Carrie Murray—Steve's wife
Caryn Shipley—Matt's old love interest
Wilson Delamar—Margot's worthless father
Dorothy Delamar—Margot's self-centered mother
Annie-Ann Delamar—Margot's older sister (deceased)
Chief Marshall—Chief of Police, James City County, Virginia

Chapter 1

The big man stumbled down the embankment to the James River. He pitched several times as his feet became entangled in the tall marsh grass. His balance was further impeded as he grasped the handle of a heavy metal toolbox containing an assortment of rusty, clanking tools.

Noah was clumsy and slow and his speech often garbled, but what he lacked in mental ability, he made up for in his love for animals. And he had a special affinity for the wildlife of the wetlands.

"Uh oh. Watch de grass. Almost down de hill," he muttered to himself.

Noah finally made it to the sandy river beach. The James River is a tidal basin, and it was low tide. An old wooden rowboat tied up earlier at the water's edge was now resting on the bank of the river.

"Uh oh. Low tide. Now lemme see."

Moving the oars aside, Noah placed his toolbox in the boat. He untied the rope that moored the boat and pushed it through the sand. Grunting audibly, he slowly inched the boat toward the water. The stern finally made contact with the river, and the boat tossed in response to the current. Poor coordination hampered Noah's effort to climb into the bobbing boat, yet he was undaunted by the fact that he could not swim. In fact, he did not even wear a life vest.

"Still boat. Whoa…" he continued his one-man dialogue. "Now whoa boat." The boat continued to tilt from side to side, as Noah simply toppled into the boat and took his place on the wooden seat.

"'bout time, boat," he said.

Noah's big arms lacked coordination but they were quite strong. It took little effort for him to use the oars as leverage and push the boat off the shallow bank into deeper water. He pointed the boat in the direction of an inlet about a half a mile down the river. The bow of the boat passed gently through the early morning fog as he rowed swiftly past docks and coves moving with intricate knowledge of this river. The mist that floated above the water created an eerie scene, but Noah was not intimidated. This was his place. Being mentally challenged had not prevented Noah from acquiring a studied knowledge of the wetlands and its marvelous creatures. He knew where the Canadian Geese laid their eggs. He observed the ospreys as they built their nest of brush and small tree branches upon the river markers. He tossed bread crumbs into the air as gulls squawked and competed for the handouts. He knew every inch of the James River and its swamps in James City County, Virginia.

The sound of the ferry's foghorn pierced the morning air as Noah turned the boat into a cove and straight for a bevy of white, styrofoam buoys wafting in the water. The buoys marked the location of wire crab pots that rested on the muddy river bottom. As the boat drifted toward the buoys, Noah reversed the oars and held them motionlessly.

The boat slowed and came to a stop beside the first white buoy.

Noah reached for the buoy and grabbed the line that was attached to it. He pulled the rope slowly until a wire cage appeared. Inside were three crabs and a partially devoured fish. Noah reached for the metal toolbox and opened it. Grasping a rusty screwdriver, he disengaged the wire hook at the top of the pot. From inside, he gently retrieved a very large crab. He examined the crab carefully.

"You okay, little fellow?" he asked with a smile. But instead of keeping the crab, he released it back into the river and watched as it disappeared into the brackish water.

"Guess you can just go head. Now let's see what…"

His solitary dialogue was interrupted as the sound of an engine purred softly in the distance and headed in his direction. Noah strained to identify the boat through the thick veil of mist that concealed it. It was obviously moving very slowly so a collision was unlikely, but Noah still seemed unnerved by its approach. The bow finally emerged from the fog, and relief swept across Noah's face.

"Hey there. Didn't know you be here." A smile brightened the childish man's face. "You fishing?"

Noah did not wait for an answer to his question. He turned and reached into the crab pot again. As he bent forward to grab another crab, the boat began to pitch and toss. He turned a terrified face toward the occupant of the other boat. The boater stood upright clutching an extended boat hook. He was using the boat hook to jostle Noah's boat. First a few teasing bumps, then the jolts became savage. Terrifying.

"Don't do that. That not funny. I can't swim," Noah screamed. The boat pitched wildly. Noah dropped to the bottom of the boat and clutched its sides frantically. "I can't swim," he repeated.

His attacker raised the boat hook and slammed it down upon his knuckles. Noah screamed and bolted upright causing the boat to tilt wildly. His tormentor caught the side of the boat with the hook and shook it violently. Noah was tossed overboard and disappeared beneath the brackish water.

The assailant waited. With his boat hook poised his eyes searched the water around the boat. Only ripples, bubbles. Then suddenly Noah's head exploded from the river. "Help me. Please help...." He raised his arms to grasp the side of the boat. The boat hook crashed down upon his arms and hands. Once. Twice. A sickening cracking sound resonated through the humid predawn air.

"Wait. Please. Why are you doing this? I can't swim." Noah's head disappeared again into the river he loved and knew so well. Seconds later his body surfaced again. But this time there was no movement as he floated slowly to the surface, a few bubbles trailing. The murderer grasped Noah's shoulders and pushed him forcefully down.

The attacker waited his eyes searching the water around the boats and buoys until he was satisfied that the body would not surface. Then he raised the hook and slammed it downward again and again gouging enormous holes in the bottom of Noah's boat. The wooden vessel immediately began to fill with water. Then it sank slowly, slowly until it rested upon the murky river bottom.

The fog was slow to dissipate. The ferry foghorn signaled yet another twenty-minute trip across the river from Jamestown to Surry, Virginia. The assassin started his boat engine and casually moved out of the cove and disappeared into the fog.

Chapter 2

For ages the river, in which Noah Murray met his untimely and violent demise, has been the site of death and eternity for many unfortunate souls. The Powatan and other tribes of Native Americans inhabited the river region for centuries. They built their "yehakins" or huts along its life-giving banks. They enjoyed a lifestyle that relied upon the contents of the river and the resources of the surrounding swamps and forests. They made their clothing from animal skins and grasses, and they used stones for tools and weapons. And when death made its claim, they believed that their spirits were freed there on the banks of the briny river.

So when three magnificent "canoes" with white "wings" sailed up the James River in 1607, the native Americans were in awe and fearful. From the ships, named Discovery, Godspeed, and Susan Constance, one hundred and four English settlers disembarked to touch land for the first time in four and a half months on the banks of the James River. They came looking for gold and a passage to the Orient but found instead disease, famine, and death. They quickly built thatched-roof homes and called their settlement Jamestown in honor of their English King James I. Then they began their disappointing explorations. No gold was found. No passage to the Orient discovered. So they resorted to industrial and agricultural endeavors. These too were unsuccessful. Then, the natives introduced them to a strange plant that thrived along the banks of the river. They'd finally discovered a product that they could sell back home in England. They called the plant tobacco. So the settlers decided to stay in this country and raise this profitable plant, and when they died, the sandy banks of the James River provided them with an eternal-resting place.

While representing Britain's strong hold in the New World, Jamestown burned three times. After the third fire, perhaps the settlers simply became weary of rebuilding the settlement and decided not to rebuild again. Instead, a city was built just a few miles down the road. They named it Williamsburg after their King William III, and it became the capital of the Virginia colony. By colonial standards, Williamsburg presented a cosmopolitan atmosphere with its trades people, public officials, slaves, and patriots. It was here that the citizens began to dream of freedom and equality apart from their mother country, England. Soon the revolutionary spirit was kindled, and young planters and tradesmen convened on the capitol ground at the end of Duke of Glouchester Street to volunteer for the patriot cause. But their wives and mothers sensed a harbinger of death and hardship for their loved ones, and their premonitions soon spread to other women in the city and onto the plantations along the river. And when their dreadful portents came true, many young patriots were brought home to be buried on the banks of the James River.

In colonial days, establishing a plantation along the beautiful river was not merely an aesthetic decision it was also a practical business consideration. Rivers were natural highways for the planters and were used to transport agricultural products to market. It also served as transportation for the citizenry. And it was here that plantation owners, tenants, and slaves faced eternity as equals on the sandy banks of the river.

So for centuries anguished cries have resonated along the harsh shore of the James River as Native Americans, settlers, patriots, and colonials mourned the death of their loved ones. And tonight lamentations for Noah Murray floated down from Berryhill Plantation Mansion and mingled with their ancient dirges in the thick air above the James River.

* * *

Berryhill Plantation had been in the Pellinger family for two hundred years, and Einer Pellinger always welcomed guests with the hospitality customary of an influential Virginia gentleman. Tonight family members gathered at Berryhill Mansion to comfort each other following Noah Murray's funeral. Noah's cousins Matt Murray and Margot Pellinger struggled to comfort his mother, Peedee Murray.

"Noah. My poor son, Noah. It just breaks my heart to think of him dying that way. What a horrible accident! He loved the river. But try as he did, he never learned to swim." Grief-stricken Peedee paused and lifted a lace handkerchief to her face.   Then raising her silver wire-framed eyeglasses, she lightly touched each eye.

Everything about Peedee Murray attested to her gentility. She looked to be in her late sixties. Her perfectly manicured nails were tipped with mauve polish, and her long fingers were adorned with antique rings passed down from ladies of other generations who once brandished them at balls, receptions and cotillions. Her stylishly coifed hair was arranged in soft gray curls that gently framed her round, pudgy face. Through a thin application of make-up one could detect clear, delicate skin that had not been tinted by the sun nor desecrated by deep wrinkles. Her graceful hand moved the handkerchief slowly down her neck and a finger slipped discretely into her cleavage to absorb drops of perspiration that threatened to spoil her pristine appearance.

Her snappy voice flavored with a Virginia Tidewater accent continued, "Noah brought happiness to so many people, and he always did what he thought was right. He even tried to save all kinds of little creatures. Why he even tried to protect crabs. I can't think of anyone who loved crabs as much as Noah did."

"Hell, I can."   The interruption came from the direction of a high-back Queen Ann chair covered with a lavish tapestry pattern. Its occupant was a chubby man in his late fifties. A narrow crop of coarse white hair outlined his shiny, bald dome, and he wore an expensive dark blue silk suit that was completely free of wrinkles in spite of the hot humid September weather. A yellow tie lay on his crisp white shirt providing just the proper contrast of color to his otherwise conservative attire. He held a large high ball glass filled with bourbon on the rocks. A tiny drop of condensation dripped onto the tie, the only blemish on the clothing of this otherwise perfectly groomed gentleman. Seemingly oblivious to the spot he continued, "Sure, there are lots of people who *love* crabs. They love them for lunch, for snacks, for dinner…"

" Ohhhh."

Einer Pellinger's comments were interrupted by a loud swoon emitted by the near-prostrate Peedee. As the older woman fanned her face with her damp handkerchief, Margot Pellinger rose and moved quickly across the room. Like her Aunt Peedee, Margot possessed all the trappings customarily associated with women from wealthy old Virginia families. An occasional gray strand showed uncontested through her golden blonde hair that was pulled back and pinned in a bun at the nap of her neck. Like Peedee she wore little makeup choosing instead to reveal the natural beauty of her delicate fair skin. A string of perfectly matched pearls and earrings comprised her entire choice of accessories for the simple black dress she wore.

Margot spoke with a slow, soft, authentic Tidewater accent…an accent that was quickly vanishing as tourists and retirees introduced inflections and dialects from other parts of the country into the local vernacular. "Oh, Aunt Peedee, please don't. You said yourself that Noah wanted everyone to be happy. Just think how sad he would be to see *you* crying. Come on, dear. A nap would do you a world of good." As she spoke, Margot coaxed Peedee out of her chair and towards the staircase.

Noticing the spot on his tie, Einer dabbed clumsily at it with a crumpled cocktail napkin. After a few minutes he turned to Matt and said, "I always thought it was fashionable for a family to have at least one little cuckoo in the nest, but this family has a whole damned flock of them. Besides it's true what I said about crabs. Crabs are *loved* around here. They are a popular choice of food. Damnedest thing in the world for that boy to try to save crabs and make pets out of them. Yes sir, poor old Noah spent most of his time trying to prevent crabs from becoming someone's dinner. And what happens? He almost ended up being *their* dinner."

15

"Einer Pellinger, how can you talk of Noah's avocation in such an insensitive way? Especially in front of Auntie Peedee," Margot said as she reentered the room.

Einer eyed her indulgently. "You're right, of course, Dear. I keep forgetting that Peedee does not seem to view Noah's little hobby as being eccentric. However, I would venture to say that Peedee really did not view *any* of Noah's behavior as eccentric regardless of how unusual it was."

"Well, yes. Auntie Peedee has always been quite non-judgmental. But we must be careful now. Peedee suffered a tremendous shock, and we wouldn't want to put her over the edge as they say," said Margot.

"And which edge would that be, Margot?" Margot ignored Einer's jab.

During the course of this conversation, Margot's cousin, Matt Murray, had been sitting quietly by the window absorbing the view. French windows in the library of Berryhill Plantation Mansion displayed a breath-taking view of a lovely English-style garden. It was a formal terraced garden with neatly trimmed English boxwoods. A pebble path curved past beautiful flowerbeds and ornamental scrubs and sloped gently down a hill ending on the bank of the James River. A variety of century-old trees surrounded the garden providing a lush green backdrop. The setting sun was reflected in the river and a mist rose slowly from the golden water. An osprey bleeped as it winged its way to its nest that was nestled securely on a river marker and protected by wildlife laws. A breeze stirred the mist, swirling it upward as it took on an almost human shape. Tall grass along the riverbed rustled, and a dank smell of the wetlands filled the room. Matt Murray breathed deeply. He was home again.

"Matt. Matt Murray." In response to Margot's soft but commanding voice, Matt turned to face his cousin. "Matt, I am so sorry that your trip was tainted by this unspeakable accident. How unfortunate that on your first trip home since your mother died, you are faced with yet another family death."

"Yeah, it's unfortunate, Margot. Unfortunate in the sense that Noah's dead. More unfortunate yet that he died the way he did. He was Aunt Peedee's reason for living since Uncle Will's death. This has got to be heart-breaking for her, and it'll present a real hardship for you, too, since you're her closest relative still living in Williamsburg."

"Closest and only. Of course Steve lives over in Portsmouth," Margot added as she moved toward the bar. "But then Auntie Peedee will need a woman now won't she? Matt, could I serve you some sherry?"

"Hell, Margot," Einer interrupted lifting his empty glass and rattling the ice cubes, "If you're going to offer the man a drink give him a real drink, not that damned wimpy stuff."

"Einer Pellinger! Now you watch your language. I think you have already had your limit this evening. Matt, what can I get you?" Even when reprimanding Einer, Margot's voice barely rose above a whisper.

"I'll join you in a glass of sherry, Margot. I have to drive this evening."

"Huh!" Einer scoffed. Matt smiled.

Margot reached for a cut glass carafe filled with a rich honey colored liquid. She removed the stopper and poured a generous portion of the liquid into an exquisite crystal sherry glass. She handed the glass to her cousin, and settled onto a stool beside him. Margot raised her glass slightly and murmured, "To happier times."

Matt lifted his drink and responded, "Yes, to happier times."

The two sipped the warm drink silently allowing it to quell their grief at the death of their cousin. Margot appeared not to notice Einer as he pushed himself from his chair and moved unsteadily toward the bar. He reached for a bottle of bourbon and skeptically examined its half-empty contents. Shrugging, he added an ice cube and filled his glass with the amber colored liquid. Almost as an after thought, he reached for a bottle top and added a capful of water, just enough to validate his claim that he was a B & B man. Then he sauntered back to his chair.

Margot ignored his comment and moved closer to her cousin. "Matt remember when you and Steve invited Hank Wilson, and Annie-Ann and I invited Caryn Shipley for a weekend trip to the Outer Banks. We stayed with Grandma Murray in her old summer cottage. Noah was always there. And Matt, remember how primitive the old cottage was. Long after Grandma Murray got town water, we still used the old pump on the back porch. And we'd pass the blame if someone forgot to leave water in the dipper for priming it the next time. That water was so much colder than what came from the faucet."

"Yeah, Grandma Murray used to tell us that she kept a block of ice under the porch to keep the pump water cool for us."

"He was certainly kind. I'll never forget when I first realized Noah was different from the rest of us. I was just a little kid. We were over on the Outer Banks at Grandma Murray's cottage and a bunch of kids surrounded Noah and made fun of him. They grabbed his glasses, covered the lens with sand, and stuck them back on his face. Not only was he unable to see, but he also had sand in his eyes and a big scratch on his cheek. Noah was yelling at the top of his lungs, 'Why are you doing this to me? I like you. Why don't you like me?' He was, of course, drooling and they taunted him for that, too. They called him Mad Dog and Slobber-Puss. I was just a little guy and didn't understand why they were doing this to my big cousin that I thought was so great. I ran as fast as I could screaming for Grandma Murray. Grandma flew down the steps with a broom in her hand, and raced down the road as fast as her legs could carry her. She got in a few solid whacks, too. Then she caught this one guy, who had been the main tormentor, and dragged him to her back porch and had him, wash Noah's glasses. Then she made him apologize to Noah. Poor Noah was bawling so loud that he couldn't hear him." Matt paused. "Grandma Murray surely defended Noah. Anyone who ever made fun of Noah around Grandma Murray lost a friend for life."

"Oh don't, Matt, please. I can't bear to think of those incidences. I prefer to remember how kind and gentle Noah was. He was such a wonderful part of my childhood. You could tell him anything, and he never betrayed a confidence. And patient. Why I'll never forget how jealous I was when you and Steve learned to street skate. I would know no peace until I learned too. Me, the clumsiest girl in the second grade," she chuckled. "I tried and tried until my knees were a mass of scabs and scrapes. One day I was so frustrated that I sat on the curb and let the tears flow. You and Steve just rolled off, but then there was Noah. He stretched his hand out to me and said, 'Don't cry Margot. I

19

won't let you fall no more.' I just reached up and took his hand, and I knew that I wouldn't fall again. Noah held my hand and kept me from falling until I learned to balance myself. Then he was as happy as if *he* had learned to skate. He said, 'Good job, Margot. Good job!' the way he always did. Then he clapped and laughed so hard that those old thick glasses slipped down on his nose so far that I thought they'd drop off."

Matt smiled and nodded. "Yeah, Noah certainly was gentle. He meant the world and all to Aunt Peedee, Uncle Will, and Grandma Murray. I know he felt loved and special." He paused and patted her hand. "You were special to him, too, Margot. Of all his cousins, he would always go to you first."

"Thank you, Matt," her voice was almost a whisper. "I did try to be there for him. But I must admit that there were times when I made excuses of doing other things when he called. And do you know what? He would always say, 'That's okay, Margot. Catch you later.' Then I'd feel guilty. I will say, however, that I always made an effort to make it up to him. Usually I'd take him for a ride in one of our powerboats. He liked to go fast. He said it made him feel like a sea gull soaring through the air. Sometimes we'd go down to see the James River Reserve Fleet. He was intrigued that the discarded ships in storage there were called 'the ghost fleet'. He thought it was so sad to see these massive steel ships just rusting away. And he was concerned that the rust would affect the river water and harm the wildlife, too. A few years ago, a junked freighter leaked oil into the river. Noah was beside himself with concern. He wanted to repair all the ships so they wouldn't leak any more. You know Noah. He wanted to take care of everything… the environment, the wildlife, and even old rusting ships. Oh, Matt, I miss him so much."

Matt reached out and squeezed Margot's hand. "He knew we loved him, Margot. Now I've got to go. Steve will wonder where I am since the funeral. I'm afraid that he still thinks of me as his little brother."

Matt stood and kissed his cousin on her cheek. He walked to his host's chair and extended his hand. Einer positioned his hands on the arms of the chair in an effort to lift himself. Realizing his attempt might not be successful, Matt bent down and grasped his hand. "Please don't get up, Einer. Goodnight."

* * *

Matt slowly drove the Ford Blazer down the coach road from Berryhill Plantation Mansion. He felt a deep sadness after attending his cousin's funeral, and he felt tremendous regret at not having seen him for so many years. Noah was a part of Matt's past, his history. Noah was one of the tribe. The whole family gathered ranks to protect and love him. Not because they pitied him but because he was one of them. He was patient and compassionate and other people tended to take on these qualities by virtue of simply being around him.

Matt reached the main road and turned right onto John Tyler Highway. He dimmed his headlights as a car approached. As the car passed, he read the words, James City Police Department. His eyes went up to the rear view mirror, and he saw that the vehicle was signaling a left turn into Berryhill Plantation. Should he go back? No. He reasoned that since the police car had not been using its emergency lights, that this wouldn't be a crisis visit. Besides he was exhausted.

Chapter 3

Margot quietly closed the door behind Matt. She stood silently for a few moments with her back against the massive mahogany door. Then she breathed an audible sigh and moved across the grand hall. Einer had not stirred. He was slumped in his chair and his coat, once wrinkle free, was now crumpled around his belt. He held his half-empty glass precariously over the expensive Oriental rug. Margot gently lifted the glass from his hand and stood silently as Einer stirred. When he again lay motionless, she busied herself about the room placing glasses on the bar to be washed by the maid the next morning, picking up magazines, and sorting newspapers. Her eyes fell upon the bold print in the bottom left-hand column of the Virginia Gazette, *Local Man Drowns*. She quickly folded the paper as if concealing the headlines would make the dreadful events of the past few days vanish.

Margot turned her attention to her husband who was obviously unable to climb the stairs. Why hadn't she asked Matt to help her put him to bed? Pride. She answered her own question. The family was aware of Einer's occasional night drinking binges, and they were aware that lately the sessions often carried over into the next day. Peedee once chided Einer for carrying about his own "libation" in a silver flask. In spite of his drinking, there was never any doubt that Einer worshiped Margot. After having too much to drink, Einer's declarations of love became trite and effusive. He'd laugh loudly and hug her close to him. To

Einer Margot was still the younger woman adored and pursued by the widower Pellinger. When Einer's first wife died, he observed a respectful grieving period, and then he met Margot. After a brief but flamboyant courtship she agreed to marry him, and in spite of their age difference Margot's love and devotion to Einer appeared unquestionable. Consequently, family members neither advised nor interfered in their relationship. They just watched silently as his drinking steadily increased.

Headlights swept the room as a car slowly made its way up the unpaved carriage road to Berryhill Mansion. Moving to the window, Margot drew the curtain aside and peered out at the approaching vehicle.

"Oh dear," she said softly as she spotted the words on the car that read James City Police Department. She moved swiftly across the room and softly closed the library door behind her. There was the sound of footsteps as the callers climbed the steps to the front porch. These were followed by the toll of the Windsor door chimes. Margot flew across the hall and threw open the door in an effort to thwart a second tolling of the carillons.

"Oh, good evening, Audrey, Donald." Margot addressed the two young, uniformed officers. Audrey and Donald attended school with Margot, and they were curious when their assignment required them to come to Berryhill Plantation. They had heard much about their old classmate's opulent home and were anxious to see inside. Berryhill was one of the few plantations on Virginia Highway Route Five not open for public tours. The house was secluded behind a thick stand of pine trees and brush, concealing it from the main road, John Tyler Highway. Berryhill had a spectacular and intriguing past that predated the Revolutionary War. And as happens with so many old mansions, it had gained a reputation for eerie happenings.

"Good evening, Margot," Audrey replied. "I apologize for coming by so soon after Noah's funeral, but there's very important information I need to notify you and your family of. I understand Mrs. Peedee... uh...Penelope Murray is staying with you tonight."

"Why, yes, she is Audrey. We felt it best that she not be alone for awhile. She is, of course, grieving."

"I see," the detectives shuffled nervously.

"Oh, please forgive me Audrey, Donald. Won't you come in?"

Margot opened the door wide and stood aside as the two detectives entered the hall. Audrey and Donald gawked as they stepped into the luxurious interior. Eighteenth century Berryhill Plantation was built of brick fired by slaves right on the plantation. The Georgian mansion contained handsome woodwork and arches throughout the house. A hand-carved staircase graced the grand entrance hall and spiraled up to the second story. They had heard there was an entire third floor that comprised a lavish ballroom once used to entertain neighbors, statesmen, and perhaps even heads of state. Peering through doorways to adjoining rooms, they caught glimpses of original paintings, silver, and antique furniture that adorned the house. The police officers had never conducted an interview in such a grand setting.

"Follow me, please," Margot moved toward the parlor across the hall from the library. Audrey noted the closed door to the library but said nothing.

"Won't you sit down?" Margot gestured toward an antique sofa covered with a rich green velvet fabric and flanked by matching parlor chairs. The detectives sat on the sofa and Margot chose one of the chairs. "Now may *I* help you, Audrey?"

"Margot, it would really be best if Mrs. Murray and your husband could be here. What I have to say is very important and will concern you all."

"I see," said Margot. "Well that is not possible at this time. I gave Aunt Peedee a mild sedative. She's sleeping now. For the first time in days I might add. So you see, I don't dare disturb her."

"Uh…," said Donald. It was the first time he had attempted to speak and his voice cracked. Even in high school, Margot intimidated him. He cleared his throat. "Ah…how about your husband, Margot? Could we speak with him?"

"No, Donald. Mr. Pellinger is --well, indisposed at the moment. I am sure he would be glad to talk with you in the morning. If you could just tell me what this is all about then perhaps I could help you."

Audrey suppressed a smile when Margot referred to Einer as *Mr.* Pellinger. She said, "Margot, as you know the medical examiner did a careful examination of Noah's body after it was found. An autopsy." Margot gasped.

"Surely you knew that," Audrey stated simply.

"Yes, yes. I supposed such but the word autopsy sounds so brutal." She shuddered.

"It's routine when someone dies of unnatural causes. Noah's autopsy was not unusual in that sense. When we found Noah's body…"

"Oh, please," Margot interrupted. "Could you just say found Noah? Not found Noah's body. Body sound so impersonal."

Audrey concealed her growing impatience, but she was beginning to wonder if Margot was deliberately trying to thwart the interview. "Sorry. When we found Noah there were several things that looked suspicious to us. However, we didn't want to say anything until after the au...after the examinations were complete. Besides we knew your family was busy with funeral arrangements and all."

"Thank you. Yes, we had just about all we could handle the last few days. Thank you for that consideration, Audrey," Margot said.

"But now that the funeral is over," picking up the conversation, Donald blurted, "we've gotta talk to Noah's family. You see, Margot, we have evidence that indicates that your cousin was murdered and the body was disposed of in such a way as to make it appear that he drowned while trying to dump crabs from someone else's pot."

The room fell silent. The eyes of both detectives were glued on Margot. She touched her trembling finger together and slowly raised them to her lips. Then she spread her fingers and covered her mouth as if to silence a cry. No sound came.

"Margot, are you all right?" asked Audrey as she moved quickly and knelt by her chair.

Silent tears streamed down Margot's face. She whispered, "Why? Why would anyone want to *murder* a kind, gentle person like Noah? There must be a mistake, Audrey. You know how he was. Who could hate him? I can't believe it."

"Are you sure you don't want to call your husband in, Margot?"

"No. Please don't. I'll be fine. It's just the shock of the whole thing." Margot lifted her head and dried her eyes with a white linen handkerchief. Margot rose slowly but steadily. "I'll be sure that Mr. Pellinger gets this urgent information, and I know he'll see you first thing in the morning. Mr. Pellinger will know what to do. Noah was very dear to him. Noah was very dear to us all."

Margot moved to the door and through the hall. She opened the front door and turned to Audrey and Donald. "It is always so good to see someone from our high school class. I'm just sorry it had to be under these horrible circumstances. Thank you for informing us. I'm sure that Mr. Pellinger will apprise the whole family of all your findings as soon as he talks with you. Good night."

The two detectives stepped outside and muttered good night. When they reached the car Audrey confronted Donald. "Hey that was real stupid in there Donald. Real insensitive the way you just threw it out about Noah being murdered and someone trying to make it look like he drowned while emptying a crab pot. Yeah, real insensitive to Margot's feelings."

"Hey what'd I do?" Donald said in an effort to defend himself. "I was just trying to give her the facts. You know, let her know what really happened."

"You got to learn to temper it, Donald. Temper it," repeated Audrey as she climbed into the car. "At least, until we think we got a suspect. Before we got the autopsy report back, we were conducting a quasi-official investigation. Now that we know for sure it was murder, this is the real thing. The real thing, Donald. So don't go screwing it up by alienating family members." She slammed the door hard.

* * *

Margot closed the door softly. She couldn't stop sobbing. She ran to the library door and threw it open. Racing across the room, she knelt by Einer's chair. She took his hand and began to pat it. First lightly and then firmly.

"Einer. Einer. Wake up Dear." She could hardly see his face through her tears. "Something dreadful has happened. Oh, Einer, please wake up." She pinched his jowls between her fingers and shook his head. Einer slowly opened his rummy eyes. He tried to focus them on Margot but gave up and closed them again.

"Einer please I need you to help me. I need you to help Auntie Peedee. I need to know that you are going to take care of this terrible thing that has happened. Please wake up."

When there was no response, Margot's sobs slowly subsided. Finally she sat on a footstool next to Einer and simply placed her head on his chest the way she had slept so safely for so many years. As if on cue, Einer raised a trembling hand and clumsily stroked Margot's hair. "Shhhh," he whispered, "Shhhh."

Chapter 4

Matt turned off John Tyler Highway and onto John Rolfe Lane. When he reached The Maine, he turned left and headed towards his old home place facing the James River. He looked forward to relaxing this evening with his brother, Steve, and his friends Ignatius Harder and Benjamin Day. Matt's Tennessee friends, Ignatius and Ben, had accompanied him to James City County Virginia for a vacation.

Years ago, Matt had moved to Franklin County Tennessee with his young wife Jill and infant twin sons, Chad and Garth. As a young engineer at Arnold Engineering Development Center, Matt struggled to prove himself in his profession while making certain that he devoted plenty of quality time to his young family. For years, his family and job consumed his life. So when Jill died suddenly one still, hot summer day, Matt's existence suddenly became meaningless. He thought he'd go mad. He roamed the house at night and repeatedly checked to see if his sons were still breathing. He bought canned biscuits for meals and then burned them. He mixed the colored laundry with the white and ended up with pink underwear. And then his mother came from Tidewater Virginia to help. Suddenly delicious meals were prepared and on schedule. The boys got their homework and went to bed on time. Sheets were changed, and the laundry folded. Order was restored. But Matt was still shattered. Jill had been his wife, his lover, and his friend. They needed no one else.

They had each other. Now suddenly she was gone, and the void was agonizing.

Then one day his mother shooed him out of the house and suggested he take up jogging. It was on his first breathless attempt at running that he met his new neighbor, Ignatius Harder. Matt and Ignatius had much in common. Ignatius was also a widower, and he was an engineer working from an office in his house. They found much to talk about, and their meeting developed into a friendship that included invitations for dinners prepared by Ignatius himself and games of pool that stretched late into the evening. Although Ignatius was a paraplegic, he never passed on an opportunity to go fishing.

It was while fishing that Ignatius and Matt met Ben. Ben was a bachelor, who was considered quite a likely "catch" by the young women of Franklin County, Tennessee. He was a native Franklin County man complete with a broad grin, quaint aphorisms, and slow middle Tennessee drawl. He had a quick wit and a brand of humor that often disarmed the more serious-minded Ignatius, and Ben's witticisms frequently resulted into amicable banter between the two men. When Ben confided to his friends that he had always dreamed of being in law enforcement, Matt and Ignatius encouraged him to run for sheriff of Franklin County. With their support and encouragement, he ran and won by a landslide. Later, it was Matt and Ignatius who helped him solve his first case, the murder of a beautiful young woman whose body was found in a snowdrift. After Ben completed his testimony in the murder case, he sought a much-needed respite.

So the three men and Ignatius' canine companion, Pete, left in Ignatius' special-equipped van to enjoy a week of fishing on the James River in Virginia. Matt's brother, Steve, was anxious to show off his new powerboat.

The trip seemed jinxed from the beginning. Outside Roanoke, Virginia an over-heated radiator cost them three hundred dollars and a twenty-four hour travel delay. When they arrived at Matt's old home place, Carrie, Steve's wife, informed them that her husband received an emergency call from their Aunt Peedee. That was two hours earlier. When Steve returned ashen-faced and exhausted, he told them that their cousin, Noah, had been found dead in the James River in the middle of a bevy of crab pots. The cause of death was assumed to be accidental drowning.

Two days later, shortly before Noah's funeral, another unsettling event was reported on Channel 24 Weather Station. A hurricane named Jean was churning up the East Coast trying to decide whether it should die at sea or wreak havoc on the Carolinas. The latter option seemed to be the most likely.

* * *

Matt finally reached a familiar gravel driveway. Woods left undisturbed when the house was built now obscured his old home. Steve and Matt decided not to sell their mother's place when she died. After all she had not chosen to sell it when she came to Tennessee to help Matt care for his two sons. So the brothers rejected several offers from contractors who were buying property that had a scenic view overlooking the James River. They learned that these builders razed the older houses, and built expensive and more lavish places on the site. Steve and Matt could not bear to think of their mom's home being demolished.

So many memories. So much family lore. So, they decided to keep the property and use it for retreats and family gatherings.

Matt lowered the car windows and killed the motor. Closing his eyes, he allowed the sounds and smells of the woodlands to permeate his senses and wrest the anguish of the past few days from his mind. The snap of a twig, perhaps a deer. A night bird's screech, possibly an owl. Dank, earthy smells that were so familiar, so much a part of his youth. He was roused from his reverie by the slam of a screen door, followed by brisk footsteps.

"Hey Matt. Wondered where you were."

"Still worrying about your kid brother, Steve?"

"I suppose so," Steve laughed as he reached for the car door. "Everything okay over at Berryhill?"

Matt swung out of the vehicle. "As well as could be expected I suppose. I left Margot with Einer in an *immobile* condition. I started to offer to help him upstairs, but I didn't want to offend. I really worry about Margot. Einer is old enough to be her father, and with his drinking, is she okay in that relationship?"

"What? You mean her marriage to Einer? Hey, don't you worry about that for a minute. He dotes on her, and Einer is the master of her universe. Anything she wants, she gets. I don't understand it, but it works for them."

The two brothers walked slowly towards the house. "I feel real bad about Ignatius and Ben's vacation. They seldom get out of Franklin County, and it seems like this trip was doomed from the start. I hope I can spend the next few days making it up to them. Of course, fishing is the number one priority, but I thought we'd do Williamsburg one day too, and then take off to the Outer Banks." Matt appeared to be thinking aloud.

The brothers entered the house to find Carrie and Ignatius facing off across a card table. Carrie was shuffling the cards while declaring, "This time five card draw with deuces wild." She dealt and picked up her cards. Grumpy, red-haired Ignatius looked at his hand and huffed through his beard. A second huff soon followed, and he reached for the stub of a cigar and chewed on it savagely. Neither player acknowledged the two men who entered.

"Hey, Matthew," came a cheerful welcome. The greeter reclining in front of the television wore a red and white plaid shirt and denim jeans tucked inside elaborately stitched cowboy boots. He spoke with a true middle Tennessee accent, "Know you're plumb tuckered out."

"Hey, Ben. That I am," Matt replied. "What's going on with the weather?"

Matt and Steve took chairs in front of the television also. It was tuned to Channel 3, Norfolk. The weatherman reported the latest information on Hurricane Jean. The storm was on the move and would soon make landfall off Cape Lookout, North Carolina. Winds were clocked at 70 mph and it was moving in a northwest direction at 9 mph. Hurricane warnings were up along the eastern coast from the Outer Banks to Chincoteague, Virginia. He predicted that Nags Head, Kitty Hawk and Kill Devil Hills would probably feel the storm's true fury by sometime the next day. A more troubling report indicated that the path of the hurricane might possibly reach farther inland than previously predicted. A list of school closings rolled across the screen, and people in low-lying areas were warned to go to shelters on higher grounds. It appeared that Eastern

Virginia would not be spared. In fact, high winds and raging surf were already pounding Virginia Beach. The three men watched mesmerized as a sailboat was dashed against a pier.

"Got to get my boat away from that river early in the morning. It's gonna start to get choppy. Want to help?" Steve asked.

"Sure," mumbled Matt aware that the weather situation put a hold not only on fishing plans but also plans to tour Williamsburg and the Outer Banks.

So intent was Ignatius upon the poker game and the skill of his opponent, that he was oblivious to the report of the storm sabotaging their vacation plans. Steve went into the kitchen and returned with two beers and three glasses of brandy. Without speaking, he set the beers on the card table and handed a brandy to Matt and Ben. Matt thought how comforting it was to be in the company of people with whom you needn't speak in order to communicate.

When the poker game finally ended, Carrie busied herself folding the card table and chair, and Ignatius joined the men to watch the weather reports. From the corner of the room, a scruffy mass of curly white fur arose from a bed made of bath towels and leisurely scratched his ear. After surveying the group, the unclipped poodle spotted his target, ambled across the room, and in one spry jump, leapt upon Ignatius' lap. Ignatius gently scratched the dog's ear as he listened to the weather reporters. Finally when all available information was gleaned, the set was silenced and the conversation turned to the family tragedy.

Noah's death had truly cast a pall upon the men's vacation. "Steve, tell me again what you know about Noah's death," Matt said.

"Matt, there's not much to tell," his brother replied. "You know how Noah loved the wetland and the wildlife. He spent hours tromping through the swamps looking for turtles, snakes, and the likes. But he had a real obsession with crabs. You know, I think it goes back to when Aunt Peedee used to take us crabbing down at the beach. Remember how she'd take old rotten fish heads and tie them to string, and we'd put them in the shallow water and wait. And wait and wait until a crab would spot it, and Peedee would caution us to pull the head in real slow so as not to frighten the crab away. Now that slow pulling was the hardest part for us. You and I wanted to yank that string, remember? But not Noah. He'd drag that fish head so slow that I couldn't even tell it was moving. Then when it was out of the water, instead of snatching the crab up like we did, he'd pick it up real gentle like and tell it that he was going to put it right back as soon as he checked it out."

Matt nodded his head. "Yeah, I remember. It's amazing how such a big guy as Noah could be so careful and gentle. But what does this have to do with his accident?"

"It's just that Noah's fascination with crabs continued into adulthood. He had salt-water aquariums containing crabs that he thought couldn't make it in the wild. Like any of them last long around here anyway. The tanks held crabs with missing claws and broken shells. It's a real menagerie. Noah fancied himself some sort of wetlands Dr. Doolittle. Then he took his interest to a new level. He not only rescued injured crabs, he decided to release crabs from pots. That's when the whole thing turned ugly. You can imagine how the watermen felt when they pulled up their pots and found them empty. At first they thought a disease struck

36

the river or perhaps they over fished the waters. They were afraid that they had a real crisis on hand. Then one morning, a waterman pulled his boat into the creek where he'd thrown down several pots, and there was Noah. He was in Aunt Peedee's old rowboat pulling up pots and taking out the crabs. And do you know what he did?"

"No telling," responded Matt.

"He threw up his hand, gave this cheerful 'good morning', and simply said he was letting the crabs go. Well, all hell broke loose. Aunt Peedee got all kinds of phone calls. Some were pretty nasty, like she ought to put him in a cage. Lord knows she tried to explain to him that he couldn't go around releasing the men's catch because that was their livelihood. But Noah would have none of it. He said they ought to get another job, one that didn't hurt helpless creatures."

"Steve, that's real pitiful," interjected Ben in a commiserating voice.

"It certainly is. How did Aunt Peedee handle this?" asked Matt.

"Not very well. As usual, she and Margot turned the problem over to Einer. Einer pondered the situation and finally decided that the best thing to do was to get a companion for Noah. He looked for someone who would spend the days with Noah and accompany him on walks through the swamps. Steer him away from areas that had crab pots. But Noah's reputation preceded him, and finding a companion for Noah took longer than expected. In the meantime, Aunt Peedee and Margot tried to take up the slack. They went with him everywhere...or almost everywhere. One day Aunt Peedee, exhausted from the constant vigil, realized she'd overslept. She jumped out of bed discovered that Noah was gone. She and Margot rounded up all the people who work for them and searched Noah's usual haunts. When night came, they still hadn't found a trace of him."

Ignatius had been listening intently to the saga from behind a cloud of pipe smoke. "I bet Margot and Peedee were distraught," he said.

"Yeah, bet they were fit to be tied," added Ben.

"Yes, Ben. *Fit to be tied* is synonymous with distraught," scoffed Ignatius.

Steve continued, "They were frantic. Although Noah knew his way around the wetlands, his social skills were so limited. To anyone who didn't know him his behavior could appear to be threatening. He could be mistaken as drunk or on drugs. Einer called in the police, the whole family, and friends in his hunting club. Carrie and I came over from Portsmouth to help out. Search parties worked until way in the night. The next morning we started again at first light, and we searched until dark. Of course, we found no trace of him. The Virginia Gazette printed a picture and an article on the front page reporting that Noah was missing and was probably in the swamps around the creeks or river. The paper asked that hunters and fishermen be vigilant and report any possible sightings to the Police Chief of James City County. The article also revealed that Noah was of 'challenged mental capacity', and a reward was offered to anyone who could provide a lead to his whereabouts. We searched two evenings and a whole day with not one lead. When the family gathered to search the morning of the second day, the police hadn't arrived yet, and we had to wait."

"The search started from Berryhill instead of Aunt Peedee's place?" queried Matt.

"Yes, Aunt Peedee was staying at Berryhill. She was almost out of her head, and after all, Einer was orchestrating things. Besides, he wasn't about to let Margot out of his sight, and he knew she'd want to be with Peedee. Anyway, finally the police arrived late, and Einer was furious. I noticed that the officers got out of their cars almost reluctantly. I knew right off that something bad had happened. They told us that some crabbing watermen found a body in the James River. It was floating face down amongst a bevy of crab pots. Although the police wanted positive identification from someone in the family, they felt sure it was Noah." Steve paused and slowly sipped his brandy.

Ben leaned forward in his chair, his attention piqued by the discovery of the body.

Steve continued. "When Aunt Peedee heard what the police said, she screamed and collapsed. Margot appeared to be in shock. Einer was pale as a ghost. He picked up his glass and threw down a shot of bourbon, and said, 'I'll do it. I'll identify the body.' Margot jumped up, leaving poor Aunt Peedee sobbing. She was determined to go with Einer, but he forbade her saying that it would be no place for her, and she should take care of Aunt Peedee."

The men sat silently reflecting on the tragedy. Carrie wiped her eyes still red from grief.

"And, of course the body was Noah," Matt simply stated the obvious.

"Einer deserves kudos for the way he handled this catastrophe," Carrie said. She slipped closer to her husband. Steve reached down and began to massage her neck. Matt suddenly felt an incredible pang of loneliness as he watched Steve and his wife. He remembered how he and Jill had nocturnal rituals. On cool autumn nights they would cuddle in front of the television sharing a cup of hot cocoa. They'd take turns sipping the drink from a large mug they brought back from Jamaica. And when the cup was empty and the late news report over, they'd walk toward their bedroom his arm fixed tightly around her waist. Matt still felt a dismal void when he witnessed tender moments shared by other couples.

Carrie aimed the remote control at the television and clicked it on again. A map of the southeastern coastline appeared showing a green blotch covering most of eastern North Carolina and the Tidewater area of Virginia. The map key also showed that dark green meant heavy rain and rapidly rising waters.

"Steve, I wish you'd moved your boat up today," she said as numbers appeared indicating the inches of rainfall expected. Seven, ten, twelve…

"I wish I had moved it, too."

Chapter 5

Einer sat upon the unmade bed, his right ankle hoisted over his left knee. Suspended above his foot, he held a highly polished, hand-sewn leather Italian loafer. His attention was fixed upon Margot as she sat at a dressing table at the far end of the room. He watched as she slowly brushed her long shiny hair. Even after many years of marriage Einer found this routine mesmerizing. He had never quite come to terms with the fact that she was his. She was so much younger and more beautiful than he ever hoped to find in a second wife.

      For years following the death of his first wife, Einer had no desire for another woman. Then he saw Margot Delamar at a fundraiser at the Addy Aldrich Museum. She was so young and fragile. It was difficult for Einer to avoid staring at her. He may never have garnered courage to approach Margot had it not been for her father. Wilson Delamar interrupted Einer's gaze with a firm pat on the back. Einer never cared for Delamar with his fantastic bravado and dubious reputation. However, after a brief conversation about the success of the event, Einer learned that Margot was Delamar's daughter. Wilson steered Einer towards Margot and introduced them. It had not mattered that Margot's father was only several years older than Einer. Einer was so taken aback by her beauty and innocence that he hardly heard the words of introduction. Soon, Delamar slipped away, leaving the unlikely couple alone. Einer could not remember what they talked about.

He only recalled how amazed he was that Margot was receptive to him.

After a brief courtship, Einer rallied courage to propose to Margot. Much to his surprise, she accepted enthusiastically. The wedding was celebrated at historic Bruton Parish Church, and the reception that took place at Berryhill Mansion was spectacular. Einer bore the cost for the entire affair, but he had not minded. Paying the expenses assured him that Margot would have exactly the kind of wedding she wanted. They took a wedding trip to Paris, and their time alone was filled with a passion that Einer never dared dream it would be. It had not mattered to Einer that their marriage produced no children. Margot was his world. No one else need exist.

So as he watched Margot slowly brush her hair, he was greatly disturbed to notice her red puffy eyes. He had been unable to spare her the pain of Noah's death, but he most certainly intended to spare her the intrusion of a murder investigation. How dare those two detectives come to his home the evening of Noah's funeral and torment Margot with such news.

Einer slipped on his shoe and shuffled across the room. He placed his hands on Margot's shoulders and stared at her reflection in the mirror. "Margot, now I want you to put all this out of your mind today. I'm going down to the police station and take care of everything. The best thing you and Peedee can do is focus on healing. Noah's gone. There's nothing we can do about that. And you know that it would bring him great sadness if he knew the two of you were suffering. So for your sakes and in deference to the wishes of Noah, I want you and Peedee to find something to divert your attention from this tragedy. Leave everything to me."

"Oh, Einer, I know you're right," she said hugging his hand to her cheek. "It's bad enough to lose Noah, but to think someone actually took his life, makes the pain almost unbearable." She lifted her palm as Einer opened his mouth to object. "But you are right. For our sake and in reverence to Noah, Peedee and I must persist. After all, if there were indeed a murder, we must be alert if we are to be of any assistance." She laid her brush firmly on the dressing table as a look of determination crept across her face.

"That's my girl." Einer said gently squeezing her arms.

* * *

The wipers struggled to remove the opaque curtain of rain from the windshield as Einer turned his BMW right onto John Tyler Highway and headed straight towards the offices of James City Police. The rhythm of the windshield wipers was attuned to the pounding of his heart. By the time he reached his destination, he emerged from his car red-faced and rigid. When he entered the reception area, he moved slowly and determinedly toward the officer behind the front desk. The young man stood up quickly almost toppling his chair. He swallowed hard.

"I want to see the two officers who came to my house so late last night." Einer did not introduce himself. The formality was unnecessary for his was a familiar face throughout the state of Virginia. Einer was not just one of the wealthiest men in the state, but he was also a generous philanthropist and a political potentate. Many elected officials of both parties owed their political success to the support of Einer Pellinger. He was the man behind the man.

"Yes, sir. That would be Audrey Kelly and Donald Anderson." He pointed to an open door. "Want me to tell them you're here?"

Einer did not answer but walked promptly to the open door. Upon entering, his eyes swept across the sparsely furnished office. Journals and bound documents spilled from metal bookshelves that flanked the walls of the room. A large rolling chair stood behind an oak desk with a smaller chair on the opposite it. A group of four chairs were placed haphazardly in a corner of the room. Audrey and Donald were completely engrossed in documents spread upon the desk. His approach caused them to look up quickly their heads almost colliding. Ignoring the chair in front of the desk, Einer moved toward the corner. Pulling one chair apart from the others, he positioned a place of dominance and gestured the two detectives to sit. They did.

"Now you tell me what the hell is so important that you came to my home in the middle of the night and upset my wife on the day of her cousin's funeral." His command hardly rose above a whisper. His face was red.

The detectives shifted in their seats. They looked at each other and then Audrey spoke. "Actually we came to see you, Mr. Pellinger. However, your wife said you were not to be disturbed, so we talked with her."

"You still haven't answered my question. What was so important that this had to be done in the middle of the night?"

Audrey continued. "You see, Mr. Pellinger, the results of the autopsy done on Noah Murray indicates that his death was not accidental. In fact, it shows that he was murdered."

"Autopsy? Who gave you permission to do an autopsy?"

Donald rallied nerve to speak. His voice was louder than he intended. "You see, Sir, when a person dies of unnatural causes we always do an autopsy."

"So this autopsy indicated that Noah did not drown?" Einer asked.

"No sir. Noah did drown. However, the drowning was not accidental. Someone caused him to drown," Audrey clarified.

"You're sure of this? You're sure someone caused him to drown?"

"Yes, sir," the reply was in unison.

Einer arose signaling an end the to the brief conference. Towering above the two detectives he said, "I see that you have a job to do here. But make no mistake, I'll not have you upsetting my wife. No more late night visits, and no more discussions about this gruesome mess in her presence. Do I make myself clear?"

For a brief moment both detectives stayed in their chair. Then Audrey slowly push herself into a standing position which left her six inches shorter and many pounds lighter than Einer. "I'm sorry we can't make that promise," she said. "Mr. Pellinger, a crime has been committed. Your wife's cousin was murdered. In this kind of investigation we must talk with anyone who might be able to help us bring the perpetrator to justice. And your wife might possibly have such information and not even realize the importance of it. After all, we understand she frequently accompanied him when he went on the river."

Einer stood quite motionless for awhile. His breathing was labored as he realized the gravity of the situation. In a final effort to exert his authority, Einer shook his finger at the two detectives. "Don't you ever come around my wife unless I or my lawyer are present."

Audrey spoke softly, "Mr. Pellinger, one is always entitled to have a lawyer present during an interview… if it is felt necessary." She was beginning to feel more confident.

Einer turned and quickly exited the room.

Simultaneously with the closing of the detectives' door, a door labeled Chief opened and a tall lanky man hurried down the hall to their office.

"Well, how did it go?" he asked, his face etched with concern.

Audrey and Donald were still experiencing an adrenaline rush that had been necessary to deal with the likes of Einer Pellinger.

"Okay," squeaked Donald trying too hard to sound upbeat.

"Pretty rough," added Audrey drastically qualifying his response. "I hate to say it, Chief, but it was a real mistake notifying them of the cause of death last night. I had a feeling all along that it would be best to wait till morning. There was nothing to be gained of it, and we might have lost a lot of cooperation."

"I…it was felt," the Chief corrected himself, "that Mr. Pellinger would appreciate the police conducting an investigation as promptly and efficiently as possible. Men like Pellinger didn't get where they are today by waiting till morning to address crises."

"I really believe that talking to Margot, uh Mrs. Pellinger, last night is what really ticked him off. He's so damned protective of her," Donald said.

"Yes, and I am beginning to wonder why," added Audrey.

A look of concern appeared on the Chief's face. "Don't go there unless you really feel it's necessary," he cautioned. "Einer Pellinger is notoriously protective of his wife. If we jump in there too soon or even unnecessarily, we may never get another shot at her. Just take it slow and easy where she is concerned. This still looks to me like a crime perpetrated by an irate waterman. The damned fool, Noah, kept going around releasing their catch. That's enough to make somebody snap like a twig. Now tell me again what we have here," he said motioning to the documents that were spread on the desk.

The three policemen leaned over the desk examining photos that were spread there. Audrey spoke first. "Well briefly, the autopsy report indicates that the deceased had a number of defensive wounds. The right humerus, or upper arm, was broken. Something heavy was wielded to break the bone like that. The left second metacarpal bone and the right fourth metacarpal bone were completely shattered. Bruising was consistent with a heavy rounded object, such as a baseball bat..."

"Or the large end of a boat hook or the handle of an oar," Donald interjected.

"Yeah, they're possibilities," Audrey agreed. "At any rate no weapon has been found. The blows could have been struck to disable the victim and empower the perpetrator to hold him under the water. At any rate, he did drown. Other bruises on the shoulders and upper torso indicate that he was pushed and held under."

"Anything else?" questioned the Chief.

"Lots of minor scrapes and bruises that he sustained by thrashing about on the bottom of the river. Also, the fish and crabs got to him. Although, that was minimal."

"Got pictures?" he asked.

"Lots of pictures," Donald said.

"Where do you think we should go from here?" asked the Chief, testing the young detectives.

Audrey replied, "The first thing I'd like to do is find out all I can about the victim. Then I think we should start checking out who might have a motive. Already got someone questioning watermen in that area. However, I'm not convinced that this was random violence. I saw a statistic from the National Criminal Justice Reference Service. It said that eighty percent of all violent crimes are committed by someone who knows the victim. Should that be the case here, we have countless possibilities."

"Hmm. Okay, as we go into this, we move slowly and carefully. Any mistakes and we could have this thing pulled right out from under us. Know what I mean?" he said looking from one detective to the other. "So if you think the heat is on, you're right. Don't screw it up."

The Chief slammed his fist into the palm of his hand, abruptly turned, and walked out of the door.

Audrey and Donald stood motionless for awhile looking at the pictures spread upon the desk. The only sound was raindrops pelting the windowpanes. Apparently Hurricane Jean was not the only storm brewing.

Chapter 6

Wind caught the screen door and blew it banging against the house. Three breathless, rain-soaked men clad in yellow slickers scrambled to gain refuge from the rain. Pete, the white poodle, confronted the three men with ferocious yaps punctuated with four-paw leaps. After an inquisitive sniff, he wagged acceptance and trotted back to report to Ignatius that all was well. Carrie was speaking on a cell phone and motioned for quiet by placing her finger over her lips.

"Margot, I'm sorry, Steve, Matt, and Ben just stormed in from moving the boat. Now say that again." Carrie placed her finger over her unoccupied ear. A long pause. "Okay. Yes. Well, let me talk to the guys, and I'll get right back to you. Take care now." Carrie pushed the off button.

Carrie turned to look at Steve. The flesh around her lips was white and tears welled up in her eyes. "What now?" asked Steve.

"Steve, that was Margot..." she swallowed hard and closed her eyes.

Steve moved quickly across the room and took his wife's hands. "I gathered that. What, Carrie? What's happened now?"

"Last night after Matt left Berryhill, the police came out."

"The police?" asked Steve and Ignatius in unison. Ben's eyes widened, his interest heightened.

"Yes, I passed a squad car as I was pulling onto John Tyler," Matt confirmed.

Carrie continued, "It seems that when the police arrived, Einer was *indisposed,* and Aunt Peedee had taken a sleeping tablet and gone to bed. The detectives then proceeded to talk with Margot about developments that require further investigation into Noah's death."

"Further investigation?" Ignatius jumped in.

"What kind of developments?" asked Ben.

"Developments that indicate that Noah's death was not an accident. Developments that appear to confirm that Noah was murdered," Carrie said.

"Damn! Why didn't I go back last night when I saw the police car turn onto the coach road?" Matt asked of himself. "And Margot had to talk to them alone? Of course, Einer couldn't even stand up. Why didn't I go back?"

"Now don't go beating up on yourself, Matt," Steve consoled. "You had no way of knowing what was up."

"Yeah, but I should have. No good ever comes from a late-night police visit like that. I was just so damned tired. Some excuse, huh?"

"Well, if Matt can get over feeling guilty for awhile, I'd like to know exactly what developments the police were talking about," Ignatius said impatiently in an effort to return the subject to Noah's death.

"Margot didn't know the specifics," answered Carrie.

"Does Einer know about this?" asked Matt bitterly. "Or, is he still sleeping it off?"

Steve said, "Now, Matt. You don't understand about Einer. He may drink too much, but never...I repeat never has he let Margot down. Hell, Matt, he'd kill for her." They all looked shocked. "Poor choice of words. Don't take that literally."

50

"What's going on over there now?" asked Ignatius, again returning the conversation to the crisis at hand.

"As usual, Einer has taken over," said Carrie. "He left Margot and Peedee at Berryhill with instructions to put the whole tragedy out of their minds for the day. Said they should do that in deference to Noah who always wanted his people to be happy."

"Sounds to me like that's damned good advice," Ignatius said looking squarely at Matt.

"Sure does, Matt. Can't do much to help if you burn it out this early in the investigation. Believe me, I know." Ben spoke confidently.

Carrie continued, "Now Einer has gone to the police station to see what the hell's going on."

Matt shuffled nervously. "Didn't mean to come down so hard on Einer. Guess I transferred some of the disappointment in myself to him. Seems like he's on top of things."

"Well, Einer didn't get where he is today without being on top of things," said Steve.

"Steve's right, Matt, and you really don't have to worry about Margot. It may sound foolish, but Margot and Einer are like soul mates," Carrie said fancifully.

"So was Margot just calling to let us know what's going on?" asked Steve.

"Well, that and she wants us to come over there. She wants us to be house guests for a few days," replied Carrie. Steve looked doubtful.

"It will be okay, Steve," Carrie said reassuringly. "I think Margot really needs us. You know Einer will be wrapped up in this investigation big time, and Peedee, as sweet as she is, will be very little support to Margot. In fact, she will be an added responsibility."

"Can Margot manage five more people in the house?" asked Matt.

"Well, it's not as if *Margot* has to manage. She'll just summon her help and all will be taken care of. They have three full-time employees who live there on the estate. Let me see…there's a maid, a cook, and someone who takes care of the grounds and does repairs. And then there are part-time people who come in as needed. I don't think Margot could be considered a typical housewife." Carrie turned to face Ignatius. Hesitatingly, she said, "Ignatius, there are two very nice guest bedrooms on the first floor. Uh, in case you're wondering." Carrie seemed to be embarrassed. She added, "You and Ben will be quite comfortable there."

After some discussion it was felt that fishing and sightseeing would definitely have to wait for a break in the weather anyway. So the troupe of five began to gather their things in preparation for the move to Berryhill. Carrie phoned Margot to accept the invitation. Pete, the poodle, was excited by the activity and frisked about yapping at Ignatius' every move. It occurred to Ignatius that no mention had been made of Pete.

"Carrie," said Ignatius, "what about Pete? I won't leave him behind."

"And you certainly aren't expected to," said Carrie smiling. "People at Berryhill love animals. You couldn't be a friend of Noah's and not love animals. Pete comes with us, and he can sleep in your room. Margot says."

After they were packed, Steve, Ben, and Matt made dashes to the van carrying their belongings. When they were all ready to make the final sprint Steve said, "Carrie, don't forget to check the lights and appliances. We can't run back and forth when the weather gets worse."

"There's no need, Steve," answered Carrie, "our electricity and phone went an hour ago. That's why I was talking with Margot on the cell phone. Everything's still on at Berryhill though."

"Oh, Geez," Steve exclaimed as he lifted the hood of his slicker and darted for the van.

* * *

The rain fell steadily as the five of them drove down John Tyler Highway towards Berryhill Plantation. Berryhill was one of many plantations lining the James River. Today, few of the estates are working plantations. They serve mostly as exhibits for tourists who delight in hearing stories of the glamorous days of hoop skirts and grand balls and cringe at stories of the indignities suffered by the slaves who were the true workers of the land. But the stories the tourists like to hear most are ghost stories...tales of unrequited love; of brave heroes who died on the battlefield and returned to haunt their home place; of the ghostly laughter of children coming from far off empty rooms.

It's not that they think more ghosts inhabit the plantations along the James River than in other places, it's just that the locals feel they are more aware of them. It is believed that if you listen long enough, you develop an instinct. For generations they have listened to the sounds of the river and swamps and have come to accept their spectral presence. So when the wind plays tricks in the old plantation mansions, and the haunted shores of the James River are covered with mist and river fog, and a room suddenly goes cold, locals don't understand why tourists can't sense their ghostly presence, too.

Following Matt's directions, Ignatius turned off John Tyler Highway and onto the coach road leading to Berryhill mansion.

"Hey Ben and Ignatius, get ready to be awed," said Steve as Ignatius stopped the van and peered up at the Georgian mansion.

Although Ignatius and Ben had attended Noah's funeral, they hadn't joined the family when they returned to Berryhill. So this was their first visit to Berryhill Mansion. A maid opened the enormous door so quickly in response to the peal of the door chime that the drenched guests supposed she was posted there to await their arrival. Once inside the scene was more than Ignatius and Ben could assimilate. They gawked at the grandeur of the great hall with its fine woodwork and spiraling staircase. Portraits of men showing attitude as arrogant as Ignatius stared down at the man in the wheelchair. And from gold leaf frames, portraits of women smiled coyly as the beautiful Margot descended the stairs.

"Oh, Matt, Steve, thank you. Thank you for coming." Margot moved to Carrie and brushed her cheek with a kiss. "Carrie, I can't tell you how much it means to have another woman here...well, another one other than Aunt Peedee. And Ignatius, Ben, welcome to our home. I'm just sorry that your first visit is not under happier circumstances. But we must try to make things as pleasant as possible. That's what Noah would want." She took Ignatius' rough hand in hers and simply held it. When Pete growled suspiciously, she let him sniff her hand and then scratched behind his ear. Then she extended a soft hand to Ben and smiled. His face turned red and he grinned, "Mam."

The maid returned without their wet wraps and stood unobtrusively awaiting instructions. Margot continued, "Einer says welcome, and he will be home shortly. He was so pleased that you would come. Now let me see. Maxine, if you will show Mr. Harder and Mr. Day to their downstairs rooms, I'll accompany our other guests to theirs." Margot was already ascending the steps. "Aunt Peedee will join us for drinks in the library."

Chapter 7

Dinner was exquisite. Ben sensed that the fine china and delicate crystal gracing the table was the norm rather than a setting used only for special occasions. The glow from the silver candelabrum provided an illusion of peace and serenity, and the slithering sheets of rain that slid down the panes of the French doors only served to enhance the gracious ambiance.

The meal was perfection. A salad of mixed greens was served with a raspberry vinaigrette dressing. Salmon fillets topped with dill sauce were flanked with crab cakes and accompanied by crisp vegetables and hot homemade bread. The dessert was coconut cream pie covered with chocolate sauce and dollops of whipped cream.   Ignatius, who took pride in his own culinary skills, savored every bite and made mental notes for his own cooking purposes.

Einer was a gracious host. Although surrounded by opulence, Einer sought to put his guests at ease by skillfully steering the conversation to a lighter vein. He chose topics that were pleasant, and the guests were made to feel comfortable and included. They talked about the hurricane, fishing, and local sites of historical interest. Einer offered to take Matt and his friends fishing in one of his powerboats when the hurricane passed. They talked about everything except what was on the mind of every person there…the murder of Noah Murray.   Peedee and Margot were especially quiet, and Matt wondered if there had been one minute today in which they had not thought of Noah.

After the meal was finished brandy was poured. Einer sniffed the golden liquid and rolled in about in his glass. Then he lifted his head and in a very loud voice said, "Where is that chef?"

At Einer's behest, the door to the kitchen suddenly swung open and a short, plump gray-haired woman virtually skipped into the room. A tall white chef's hat, that served to elevate her height, bobbed up and down with each spry step.

"Lexie, you did it again. Best meal yet. Now you remember this one. Want you to serve it again. Good meal. Good meal." Lexie beamed and nodded as she backed through the swinging door. Einer never failed to praise Lexie in the presence of his guests. He was sure that praise as well as a hefty salary would assure him of her continued services. She had worked for him fifteen years.

* * *

The party finished their brandy in the library. As the conversation focused on the approaching hurricane, Einer kept a watchful eye on Margot. There were circles under her eyes and her eyelids began to droop. Soon he suggested that she retire. Peedee and Carrie also felt this was a good idea, and joined Margot as she wearily climbed the stairs to the second floor.

The men sat silently as they drank brandy and listened to the rain tap steadily against the windows. Einer was restless. Soon he explained that he wanted to check on Margot. He urged Steve, Matt, Ben, and Ignatius to enjoy more brandy and even invited Ignatius to feel free to smoke his cigars and pipe. Then Einer, too, disappeared hastily up the stairs.

"Matthew, I really like old Einer," said Ben. "I must admit I was dumbfounded when we walked into this house. Never seen a place like this that folks actually live in. But you know Einer is not one bit highfalutin. He's just real folks."

Ignatius immediately reached for a cigar. Soon he was engulfed in a cloud of wretched-smelling smoke. Finally he glanced in the direction of the hall and peered cautiously up the staircase. Then leaning forward, he said in a low voice, "I agree with Ben, Matt. Einer is as regular a guy as I'd hope to meet. But where the hell has Margot been this last century while women were climbing off their pedestals and clamoring for their own identity?"

"Now I don't know, 'Natius," drawled Ben, "I think it's kinda refreshing to meet a genteel lady like Margot."

"Well, you would," replied Ignatius.

Matt lifted a finger to his lips. The four men pulled their chairs closer together and Matt replied in a hushed voice, "Ignatius, you'd have to understand where Margot comes from. I mean really comes from. Her parents are a mess. Aunt Dorothy, Margot's mother, was quite different from my father and Uncle Will. Dot, as Wilson sometimes called her, wanted more than my grandparents could give her. She wanted connection to a crowd she envied all her life. She wanted money, status, and prestige. Mostly money. My grandparents weren't parsimonious, but they were very frugal. They'd lived through the depression, and experienced all the hardships that a family struggling to raise three kids encountered. They believed in education and hard work. My dad and Uncle Will readily accepted their viewpoint, but not Aunt Dorothy. She was looking for a short cut."

Steve, interrupted, "Yeah, I remember Dad and Uncle Will saying that Aunt Dorothy was really smart. They claimed, however, that their sister was just too damned lazy to go to college and make it on her own. She was always looking for the easy way. A short-cut as Matt said."

"Yes, and she thought she'd found that short-cut in Wilson Delamar," said Matt. "Delmar is from an old Virginia Family. The Delamar name is prominent in the fishing industry. They also have a large estate on John Tyler Highway…not too far from here. Aunt Dorothy fell for Delamar's looks, his line, his name… and she thought his money."

"But," said Steve, "his family didn't fall for her."

"Yeah," continued Matt, "but Aunt Dorothy was a beautiful woman, and Wilson proposed. After the wedding, they learned why the Delmar family hadn't wanted Aunt Dorothy for their daughter-in-law. It seems their family business was in the red. The Delmars were broke, and the cost of their lifestyle greatly exceeded their income…"

"Yeah, what's that saying…a champagne appetite and a beer income," Steve added with contempt.

Matt continued, "Mr. and Mrs. Delmar had hoped that their only son would save them from financial embarrassment by marrying someone of more lucrative means. And poor Aunt Dorothy found herself as financially strapped as she was before she married."

"Didn't she actually leave Wilson once?" Steve asked.

"Oh yes, she did. Delamar was notorious for his womanizing. He and Aunt Dorothy fought so much that they made Punch and Judy battles look like a love fest. Aunt Dorothy finally left him one time, completely disillusioned. Had it not been for the death of Wilson Delamar's parents, I doubt that he and Aunt Dorothy would have gotten back together," said Matt.

"Death of his parents?" Ben leaned forward, his interest stirred.

"Yes," Matt said. "Mr. and Mrs. Delamar took a day trip to the mountains. They both died in a one-car accident just outside of Charlottesville."

"How did the Delamars' death cause Dorothy and Wilson to get back together?" asked Ignatius.

"The insurance money," replied Steve and Matt.

"Insurance money?" repeated Ben.

"You're beginning to sound like an echo, Ben," Ignatius said irritably.

Matt continued. "Yes, Mr. and Mrs. Delamar left enough insurance money for Wilson to hang on to the business, the estate, and Aunt Dorothy for a while longer."

"And hang on is what they've been doing for years," added Steve. "Lifestyle and social connection come first. Clothes, cars, club dues, the likes. I understand the house was in bad need of repair, but they kept all the accouterments that attest to a more affluent way of life….you know the paintings, silver, and all that stuff. Wilson is quite the charlatan."

"How could Margot's mother live with all that deception?" asked Ignatius.

"Oh, I'm sure she felt conflicted. For one thing, Grandma Murray constantly reminded Dorothy that she had a lot to be proud of in her own right. But expecting Aunt Dorothy to choose Grandma Murray's point of view over

Delamar social status was too much to ask. Back in the forties and fifties, it was hard for women like Dorothy to make that kind of choice," said Matt.

Ignatius said, "Well, you've told me about Margot's mother and father, but this doesn't answer my question." He repeated his question, "Where has Margot been the last century while women were climbing down from their pedestals and cultivating their individuality?" he repeated the question stubbornly.

Steve began, "Well, you see, Margot had a sister…"

"Oh, for God's sake, Steve. I got to hear another family story before I get an answer to my question about Margot?" Ignatius said in a raised voice.

"Now hang on 'Natius. Don't be so impatient," Ben whispered softly in an effort to remind his friend not to speak too loudly.

"You gotta know about Annie-Ann to understand Margot." said Matt.

"Oh, Geez. Ask a simple question and you have to listen to the entire family history," groaned Ignatius. "Annie-Ann? Who the hell is Annie-Ann?"

Steve said, "Annie-Ann was Margot's older sister. She and Aunt Dorothy were as alike as two peas in a pod. Annie-Ann liked the high life…the clothes, the dances, the coming out parties. She enjoyed the clubs and all the social connections. Like Dorothy, she was very bright but felt social connection was more important than personal accomplishments."

"And Margot?" asked Ignatius, once again trying to get an answer to his original question.

"Grandma Murray used to call Margot a knee-baby," interjected Steve. "She was just a playmate for her older sister. Choices were always made in Annie-Ann's favor. If money was tight and clothes were needed, new things were bought for Annie-Ann. Margot got used stuff. Aunt Dorothy drove to Richmond thrift shops to shop for Margot. In that way Williamsburg people wouldn't recognize that Margot wore their cast-offs. Annie-Ann's long curls were always arranged in the latest fashion. Margot had an easy-to-keep, straight Dutch boy bob. Annie-Ann had dance and piano lessons. Margot clipped paper dolls from an old Sears catalog."

"Consequently," Matt picked up the story, "Margot was very shy and awkward. She'd been taught that it was wrong to lie, but she heard her mother lie constantly about social connections, party invitations, money…mostly money. Her father lied. Annie-Ann lied. The whole family was a lie. It didn't seem to bother the rest of them. Margot never contradicted them, but she had to be confused. When she was a teenager, she gained a lot of weight. Wilson didn't make it any easier for her. He'd tease her by singing 'rolley, polley, daddy's little fatty. Bread and jelly twenty times a day.' She'd cry. As a matter of fact, Noah was her greatest defender. But Wilson wouldn't just let it go. Once when Noah was comforting Margot, Wilson said something like 'look at Rolley and her idiot pal'."

"He seemed to get some kind of sadistic satisfaction from tormenting Margot and Noah," said Steve.

"Yeah, and I thought Grandma Murray was going to kill him," said Matt.

Steve nodded, "Yeah, but Margot grew up, and she shed that weight. When she was about eighteen she turned into a knock-out! Talk about the proverbial ugly duckling!

Couldn't believe what was happening to my cousin." Steve whistled softly.

"That's when Wilson and Aunt Dorothy started dragging her to social events. For years Margot was pushed into the background. Now suddenly she was a family trophy. I understand they were ecstatic when men started paying attention to her. And she had developed quite a personality."

Steve laughed, "Yeah both of them." He cupped his hands around his breasts and thrust his chest out.

Matt ignored him. "I suppose Wilson and Aunt Dorothy's expectations were surpassed when Margot caught Einer Pellinger's eye at the Addy Adrich Museum fund raiser," Matt said.

"Einer certainly fell fast and hard. He paid for the wedding, dinner, reception, and they spent two weeks in Paris," Steve added. "Then we noticed that Delamar had a new car. The Delamar place was completely restored. Talk on the street was that Einer paid off a lot of Delamar debts, too. Seemed like old Wilson landed on his feet again."

"But what about *Margot?*" Ignatius persisted.

"Matthew, Natius is starting to get testy. Better answer the question," suggested Ben with a grin on his face.

Steve finally got to the point, "Einer's money doesn't mean a thing to Margot. It's Einer that's important to her. Einer belongs to the school of 'how can I love you today, Margot?'. Margot finally feels needed, secure, and uncompromised. She revels in the attention he shows her. Sure, her dependency on him is child-like, and I suppose it could be detrimental if his feelings for her weren't completely unquestionable. So if Einer wants to protect and indulge her, *she's* okay with that, and so is the rest of the

family. I guess I'm just glad to see Margot get her justs."
Steve took a deep breath.

"Hum..." Ignatius mused. "I suppose that makes
sense. Unusual these days, but understandable."

The three men sat silently for a few minutes. Twelve
chimes from the mantle clock reminded them why they
were so exhausted. Pete lifted his head and eyed his master.
Ignatius took two deep drags from his cigar, igniting the tip
and creating a long strip of ash. "Whatever happened to
Annie-Ann?" He asked in a sleepy voice.

Matt looked at his friend solemnly, "Annie-Ann died
when she was nineteen."

Ignatius' eyes jerked open. He was suddenly wide
awake again. "Died? How?"

"The family was vacationing at Kitty Hawk. Wilson
spotted one of the girls surfing alone. He thought it was
Margot. He ran to the beach to call her in, but she was
already in trouble. Rip tide was awful that day. She was
dashed into the pier before he could reach her. Wilson was
inconsolable. You see, Annie-Ann drowned."

Ben sprang forward in his chair. "Drowned?" he
repeated. "Her too?"

There was no response. Suddenly the steady drum of
the rain on the roof seemed sinister. The three men sat
silently and listened as the clock ticked into tomorrow.
They wondered at a family that experienced so many
accidental deaths.

Chapter 8

Audrey hung up the phone. "Well, that was Einer Pellinger. He's at Berryhill this morning and agreed to let us to talk with Mrs. Peedee Murray if we limit the interview to personal information about Noah. If it goes beyond that, he wants a lawyer there. Damn, I knew we shouldn't have gone over there the other night. It's really made him defensive." She began to pull on her slicker and continued. "So this time out, lets go by *his* rules. Only personal info about Noah. Einer Pellinger is not going to be bullied. So we'll use this trip to gain his confidence and cooperation."

Donald spoke optimistically, "At least the Chief still has confidence in us. Otherwise, he'd have pulled us off the case last night."

"Big whoop, Donald," Audrey said sarcastically. "Do you think that's why the Chief left us on this case? Because he has confidence in us? We're lowest on the food chain. The least seniority. We're dispensable, Donald. If we screw up, he figures no great loss."

"So what'll we do?" Donald asked apprehensively.

"We don't screw up," Audrey muttered.

As the two detectives stepped outside, they realized it was raining harder although the wind remained minimal. Potholes were overflowing with muddy water. Ditches crested as they ran out of places to deposit the rain. The squad car resembled a powerboat as it streamed down John Tyler Highway with breakers of water spraying from each side of the vehicle. Donald cautiously turned the car into Berryhill Plantation. Entryway to the estate was dark and

"Oh, dear me, no. Will and I never had any children. We wanted children badly. But as fate would have it, we never had any of our own. So we adopted Noah. Thanks to Einer," Peedee smiled briefly at Einer. The host raised his mug for another sip.

"Mrs. Murray, if you don't mind my asking, why do you say 'thanks to Einer'?" asked Audrey

"Oh, I don't mind. Einer's family and my family have been friends for years and years. Long before he married Margot. So when Einer learned how sad Will and I were at not being blessed with children, he arranged for us to meet Noah. He'd heard about him from one of his father's employees. Back then Einer worked for his father during his summer vacation from college. Einer has always been a caring person." Peedee smiled appreciatively at Einer.

Audrey looked at Einer. He simply nodded his head once.

"Mrs. Murray, tell us about seeing Noah the first time please. Where did this happen?" asked Audrey.

"Well…" said Peedee squinting her eyes in an effort to resurrect the memory. "We first saw little Noah at his foster parents' house. He was only three years old. They dressed him up so cute and slicked his hair back with this greasy stuff. He wasn't talking at all, and he took only a few steps at a time. But he looked at Will and smiled and stumbled right into his arms…and into our hearts." Peedee began to cry softly. Margot leaned over and hugged her aunt's cheek.

Audrey waited a few seconds. When Peedee had gained her composure, she asked, "Who were his foster parents?"

"The Rudy Birdsongs. They are both deceased now. They were an elderly couple at that time and their age prompted them to realize they were no longer able to be foster parents. I could tell how devoted they were to Noah. They were so happy when we agreed to adopt him that they wept."

Donald spoke, "Mrs. Murray, do you have any idea who Noah's biological mother is?"

"No, I don't. The Birdsongs told me that she was the daughter of a very poor man who worked for Einer's father. She died shortly after childbirth. You see, she birthed him at home, and I suppose she had no medical attention. Poor girl. I don't think anyone had a guess as to who the father was."

"Isn't it unusual for an elderly couple to become foster parents?" Audrey asked.

"I suppose they were too old for that job. But you see Noah had special needs. He was developmentally delayed. Physically and mentally he was way behind other children his age. A lot of effort was required to take care of Noah. Not many people will agree to care for a special needs child. So I suppose social services relaxed the rules a bit."

"What about Noah's school?" said Audrey.

"We enrolled Noah in a school for children who require special attention. He had physical therapy, speech, as well as an academic program suited to his ability level. Oh, the teachers loved him. He had the brightest smile and got along with all the other children. He just blossomed. Will and I knew he'd never be like other children, but he was so wanted, so loved..." Another brief interlude was required for Peedee to regain her composure.

Einer, who had remained silent during the entire interview, began to show signs of impatience. "How much longer will this take?"

"Not much longer, sir," Donald answered politely.

Audrey leaned forward and spoke softly, "Mrs. Murray, what about Noah's friends?"

Peedee lifted her glasses and dabbed her eyes. "Well, since Noah graduated from his special school, his friends have mostly been his family. Most specifically his cousins. He loved Margot. She was always so patient with him. And of course, his grandmother Murray doted on him. Let's see…," she placed her finger on her temple to enable her to think. "I could give you the names of some of the wildlife resource people who were so patient with him."

"That would be most helpful," Donald said.

"Margot, could you?" Margot anticipated her aunt's wish and left the room to get the names. Peedee continued, "Also, Noah liked to visit Colonial Williamsburg. All the interpreters knew him and were never too busy to spend time with him. Thomas Jefferson was his favorite."

"Mrs. Murray, could you give us the name of Noah's medical doctor, also?"

"Dr. Everett Harris. His office is in the medical complex on John Tyler. Do you need his telephone number?"

"Oh no, that's okay," said Audrey.

"How did Noah spend his day?" Audrey continued, fully aware of the controversy surrounding Noah's liberation of crabs.

"Oh, dear. Now there we had a bit of a problem. You see, Noah was quite tender-hearted. He couldn't bear to see any animal suffer. I'm afraid his sympathy even extended to crabs…Oh, yes." She nodded her head as if Audrey wouldn't believe her. "Noah had taken to releasing crabs from the watermen's crab pots. Einer was in the process of taking care of that problem when, when…all this happened." Peedee shivered.

"And how did you plan to take care of the problem?" Audrey continued.

"Oh, Einer was looking for a companion for Noah. Someone to accompany him to the river and the wetlands and steer him away from the crab pots."

"You've given us a lot to start with, Mrs. Murray," concluded Audrey. "Thank you so much for your time, and please accept our condolences for your great loss." She reached for Peedee's hand and shook it gently. Donald followed suit. Margot entered the room and handed Donald a list of the names of the wildlife resource personnel who had befriended Noah. As they were leaving Audrey turned and said, almost as afterthought, "Mrs. Murray, did Noah know he was adopted?"

"Oh, most certainly. We told him that his mother had to go to heaven to help God, and she knew how badly we wanted a child. So she left him with us until he could come with her." She lifted her hand to her trembling lips. "He's with her now."

Peedee began to cry again. "This has stripped my very soul," she moaned. "I'm not a vengeful person, but I do hope that this evil person will be punished in kind."

Margot knelt beside Peedee and took her hand in an effort to comfort her. "Oh, please Aunt Peedee. Don't. We have to soldier on. Remember we are going to be strong like Noah would want us to be."

$$* * *$$

Audrey steered the vehicle in the direction of John Tyler Highway. Donald was leafing through his notes and perusing the wildlife personnel list.

"Donald, make a note. We need to call Social Services when we get back to the station. See if we can get a line on this biological mother. Also, where did Einer say the out-of-town guests were from?"

"Uh, I got it here. Winchester. Yeah, Winchester, Tennessee."

"Tell you what, when we get back to the station, why don't we call the police in Winchester, Tennessee and see what we can pick up on these guys? The one in the fancy cowboy boots was staring at us suspiciously."

"Okay. Got their names right here. Just look at this," Donald said as he scratched out a reminder. "This is going to be impossible to question all these people. Is that what you have in mind? Just listen to this…" he ticked them off on his fingers, "interpreters at CW, about a dozen wildlife resource people, teachers, doctor, Social Services, and now some guys from Winchester, Tennessee. This could take weeks."

Audrey scanned both directions at the intersection, "Yes, it could take weeks if it comes to that." She turned right. "But I don't think it will. And do you know why? Because I think we've already met our killer, Donald, right back there." She jabbed a thumb in the direction of Berryhill. "You want to bet?"

Chapter 9

"Yours, too, toilet mouth," shouted the petite young woman as she slammed down the phone cracking a long red acrylic nail in the process. She swore and snatched up a cigarette. Glaring into the hall she spotted a man wearing an ill-fitted uniform. She blew a cloud of smoke upward and with a vigorous wave summoned the skinny, loose-limbed deputy sheriff. Dexter recognized the look on Penny's face and knew she meant business. He headed immediately to the glass-front door on which was printed Benjamin Day, Sheriff of Franklin County Tennessee.

"What's up, Penny?" Dexter asked, his voice etched with concern.

"What's up?" Penny repeated. Her thick middle Tennessee accent disclosed contempt. "What's up? I'll tell you what's up." She pushed her chair back recklessly and all five foot one of her unfolded. Holding her cigarette aloft and the other hand placed squarely on her hip she marched to the front of her desk. Her jeans were so tight that they appeared to be sprayed on and the white cotton knit sweater portrayed quite a sumptuous figure for such a petite young woman. She continued to blow copious amounts of cigarette smoke, and her copper colored curls bounced angrily as she marched through the haze. She stopped abruptly in front of Dexter.

"Well what Penny?" he asked again.

"Do you know who that was? Huh?" She did not wait for a reply. "Well that was some jerk-water policeman from James City County, Virginia wanting to know if we had any record on a suspicious character they are investigating in a murder case." She paused as if to make sure Dexter was following her report.

"Well, Penny," said Dexter in an appeasing tone, "You know we have to cooperate with departments in other states. Just suppose we need their help some day. It's a reciprocal thing you know."

"Oh, it's reciprocal, okay. First off do you know who told them to call *me*?"

"Well, no I don't."

"I'll tell you who. Some idiot over at the Winchester City Police Department gave them not only this telephone number but *my* name. Suggested that *I* would be just the one to help them." She tapped her highly polished boot and shook her curls in anger again.

"Were you... I mean able to help them?"

"Why yes Dexter, I was. Because do you know who they are checking up on? Do you know who the suspicious character in the murder investigation is? Can you guess?" Penny was shouting now, and several more officers skulked into the office.

"No, Penny, I sure can't," Dexter said softly. "But I think you're 'bout to tell me."

"Yes, Dexter, I'll tell you. The suspicious character that the James City County Police are checking up on is none other than our own Benjamin Day, Sheriff of Franklin County. Now how do you like them apples?"

Dexter and company looked shocked. "Penny, are you sure?"

"Yes, deputy, I'm sure. They called over to Winchester City Police first. Some clown over there thought it would be real funny if I got a call about Suspect

Day. So they told him that they *vaguely* remember hearing me speak of a Benjamin Day and suggested that he call over here and ask for me." Her voice tinged with sarcasm.

"But, Penny," Dexter said, anxiety in his voice, "do you think the Sheriff's in some kind of trouble? Maybe we should try to reach him. He might need help."

"Need help?" Penny turned on her heel and stomped back to her desk. She began to snatch up papers and bang drawers loudly. "I'll tell you who needs help. I need help. Look at all of this." She waved a hand over her cluttered desk. "The Sheriff's on vacation. No one here bothers to pick up their messages, no one turns in their time sheets, no one does nothing. And I got to put up with some smart-ass joker from over the Winchester Police Station. But you better believe I told him off."

"I'm sure you did, Penny. But what about the sheriff?" mumbled Dexter as he slowly backed out of the office.

* * *

"A sheriff? You're kidding," said Audrey as she turned left onto Strawberry Plains Road. "He stared at us so intently I naturally became suspicious of him."

"Audrey, you shouldn't become suspicious of a man just because he stared. Maybe he just liked what he saw," Donald said with a sly grin.

"Yeah, well it didn't hurt to check him out did it?" She turned into the parking lot of the professional offices.

They took the elevator to the second floor and located the office of Dr. Everett Harris. The waiting room was empty. It appeared that somehow people manage to stay well when a hurricane is moving their way. The nurse told them that the doctor would see them shortly. Fifteen minutes later Donald whispered, "I wonder how long we'd have to wait if the place was full." Ten minutes later the nurse announced that the doctor would see them now.

"I think I'll hang out here. You go on in and talk with the doc," Donald whispered to Audrey. Thinking this a bit strange, Audrey shrugged and went back to the doctor's office alone.

Doctor Harris had received a call from Einer earlier telling him that the police would be by to question him about Noah's medical history and that Peedee gave her permission for him to share any information. Dr. Harris did not question Einer's authority to give this permission. He was aware that Einer had managed Peedee's personal and business affairs since Will's death.

The elderly, gray-hair doctor sat behind a heavy oak desk and looked intently at Audrey. "Now, how can I help you, young lady?" he said.

Audrey briefly explained the purpose of the interview. Dr. Harris in turn was quite willing to answer any questions regarding Noah's medical history. Dr. Harris had been Noah's physician since he was adopted at age three. The doctor verified that Noah had been severely mentally handicapped and his physical development had been slow and tedious. It was felt that under different circumstances Noah would have been institutionalized. However, he was showered with love and attention from his adopted family and was given the best care available for children of such delayed development. Money was no obstacle, and Peedee and Will sought every resource to help Noah achieve to the best of his ability. Indeed, Dr. Harris had marveled at Noah's accomplishments and the level of independence he achieved. His general health was good, and he was even spared many childhood diseases. Dr. Harris expressed praise for Peedee, Will, and the Murray family. It was felt that without their love and support Noah would have had a pitiful life.

Dr. Harris did not know the identity of Noah's biological parents although he had heard the story that Peedee related to them. He had no reason to doubt that Noah's biological mother was the simple woman whose father was employed by the Pellinger family.

Dr. Harris had not witnessed Noah's interaction with people outside the family, and Audrey felt that these kinds of observations could be significant in the investigation. Did Noah anger easily? How did he act if he became frustrated? Was he easily accepted by others? How did he react when confronted aggressively? Dr. Harris suggested that Noah's school would be the best source for this information.

Audrey thanked Dr. Harris and shook the old man's dry, wrinkled hand. As she walked into the waiting room, she spotted Donald leaning into the receptionist's window deeply engrossed in conversation with a voluptuous dark haired nurse. Audrey shot him a frown and continued into the hall. She pushed the elevator button, and as she awaited its arrival, Donald rushed up.

"How did it go?" he asked.

"My interview went fine. How did it go for you?" the elevator door opened before Donald could respond.

They rode to the ground floor in silence. The doors parted and the detectives stepped out, and they realized the rain was reduced to a mere sprinkle. As they settled into the car, Donald said, "And so you say it went okay huh?"

"Yes, Donald, it went okay, but you haven't said how things went for you."

Donald grinned. "What would you say if I told you that for the last couple of years Margot has been bringing Noah for all his appointments?"

"I'd say go on, Donald, sounds like you didn't skip out on me."

He smiled. "Margot brought Noah to his doctor's appointments, and she wasn't always happy about spending her time with Cousin Noah. As a matter of fact, their last trip resulted in a little scene. Seems like the two of them had to wait for almost a half an hour to see the doctor. Then Noah was in the doctor's office for 'bout twenty minutes. All this time Margot was fuming. When the doctor finished seeing him, Noah came out into the waiting room and started talking with Barb, the receptionist. He was talking about crabs. Margot exploded. She said she'd wasted all morning taking him to the doctor. That he had to stop and talk to everyone…usually about crabs. And if it hadn't of been for his 'stupid obsession' they wouldn't have had to come to the doctor in the first place."

"She said that…*stupid obsession*? Why did Noah have an appointment in the first place?" Audrey said.

"Get this. He had cut his hand on a wire crab pot while he was trying to release a crab." Donald replied.

Audrey smiled. "Donald, my man, you're a treasure trove of information. Remind me to have you talk to all the cute young things from now on. Yes!"

"Is that a promise? I'm starting to like this job better and better. Where to now?" Donald said.

Audrey turned on the ignition and put the car in reverse. "Soon as I get out of the crowded parking lot, we're going to pay a visit to The Barrette School. We'll see if Noah pulled anyone else's chain." She slammed on brakes quickly as a red Camry almost backed into the car. The driver blew a whistle of relief as he realized that he'd almost collided with a police vehicle.

* * *

Everything about Barrette School said money. Newly mowed grass was thick and free of weeds. Neatly trimmed scrubs provided a lush, full backdrop for brightly colored chrysanthemums and other flowering fall plants. The circular concrete drive curved to a main door fitted with polished brass attachments and set in a sparkling glass wall. From outside one could see an infinite number of large green plants strategically placed in the reception hall to create the illusion of a tropical garden. As the two detectives entered the building, a little girl of about four moved slowly through the hall leaning forward and dragging her feet in a rolling walker. A young woman with straight brown hair and wearing jeans and a sweatshirt emblazoned with William and Mary College accompanied her. "Look at Addie, Mrs. Cox. She can really go in her new walker," the young woman said.

The receptionist looked up from her computer and smiled. "Oh, Addie, I'm so proud of you. Keep up the good work." The child beamed with pride and struggled down the hall.

The receptionist turned her smile toward Audrey and Donald. She appeared to be unaffected by the uniforms. "May I help you?"

"Yes," said Audrey. "We would like to see Ms. Simms."

"May I ask the nature of your visit?" the smile asked.

"We would like to talk to her about one of her former students, Noah Murray."

The smile vanished and her face took on an expression of sadness. "We were all just devastated to hear of Noah's death. Ms. Simms has been expecting you to call. Just a minute please. She picked up a phone and pushed a button. After a few seconds her lips moved inaudibly. Then she hung up the phone and said, "Ms. Simms will see you right away. Follow me, please."

Audrey and Donald followed the receptionist down a hallway that looked more like a museum than a school. Prints of the Masters hung in heavy wooden frames. Dispersed among the masterpieces were colorful watercolor and oil paintings displayed on beautiful mats. These paintings were obviously done by children. The exhibit was stunningly arranged on the white walls.

The receptionist stopped in front of an open door and stood aside to allow Audrey and Donald to enter. As she moved into the room behind them she said, "Ms. Simms, these are the officers to see you about Noah Murray."

Ms. Simms had a pleasant but weary face. "Come in Ms. Kelly and Mr. Anderson. Mr. Pellinger called to say that you might be by today. Please sit down." She motioned to two comfortable leather chairs placed in front of her desk. "May we get you something...coffee, tea, soft drink?"

"No thank you," the two visitors answered.

"Very well. You may go Ms. Cox. And please close the door." The receptionist left. "Now how may I help you?"

The two detectives learned much from Ms. Simms. Noah was enrolled in Barrette School as a day student immediately following his adoption. Ms. Simms had no knowledge of his birth parents. Upon entering the school, he knew few words and his physical development was extremely delayed. Although his foster parents had given him impeccable care as far as diet, clothing, and hygiene were concerned, they had not possessed the skills necessary to cultivate development in the badly handicapped boy. However, with the love and dedication of his new family, Noah surpassed everyone's expectations. It was accepted that he would never acquire the capabilities of normal children his own age, but his accomplishments were so astonishing that teachers shared the story of his progress with parents of prospective students.

Noah was classified as moderately retarded with an intellectual ability comparable to that of a five to seven year old. His rate of learning was extremely slow although he did learn to read and write a little. His speech ultimately developed well for a child of such limited capabilities. This was attributed to his enriched family and school environment. Physically he was clumsy and ungainly with very poor motor skills. His personality was bright and affable and he enjoyed meeting strangers and engaging them in conversation. He exhibited no aggressive behavior and was quite defenseless in any altercation. He was perceived to be non-threatening and strangers indulged him as he talked incessantly, usually about animals. His behavior was completely acceptable, and he achieved a reasonable level of independence. In fact until his untimely death, Noah came to Barrette School on a regular basis where he played the role of "big brother" to some of the students. He was always welcomed.

Ms. Simms' report on Noah was so complete that the detectives were left with few questions. As Audrey and Donald stood to leave, Ms. Simms added a personal note. "Noah Murray was very special to all of us here at Barrette School. We want to help in any way we can. Please know that I am available at all times."

Audrey and Donald thanked her. Donald noticed that Ms. Simms did not stand at any time during their interview. As they left the room, he glanced back to see a pair of metal crutches lying beside her desk.

* * *

"So, what did we learn from the morning's work, Audrey?" Donald was driving now and heading down John Tyler Highway toward the Law Enforcement Center.

"Nothing new, I suppose. But we did confirm a lot."

"Like what?"

She clicked off the information on her fingers. "First, we've got a cousin who resents the time she has to spend with Noah. Second, we got a husband who doesn't like for his wife to be unhappy and will do anything to please her. Third, we got a vulnerable victim who would approach anyone and strike up a conversation. Fourth, the victim's incapable of defending himself." The fingers shot up. "Confirmation, confirmation, confirmation, confirmation. And that's not bad for a few hours work."

Chapter 10

That night Matt slept erratically. He was haunted by memories of happier times with his brother and three cousins. He relished the security he'd enjoyed with Uncle Will, Peedee, and Grandma Murray. He longed for his parents. He remembered how strong and reassuring his father was, and he recalled the understanding his mother showed Steve and him. Matt found himself engulfed in despondency. The recent events left him exasperated and morose.

The old mansion was full of nooks and crannies and creaking wood. It gave forth strange noises, and he lay awake trying to identify them. After hours of wakefulness, he finally swung out of bed and stumbled to the window overlooking the garden and James River. Mist swirled above the marsh grass and wafted upward like phantoms embarked on a ghostly mission. The rain had slackened and a steady but innocuous wind stirred the branches of the trees. He pulled on jeans and a sweatshirt. Then slipping into a pair of boat shoes he moved quietly across the room and into the hall. Fragments of conversation accompanied by the delicious smell of coffee floated up the stairway.

Matt crept downstairs. He appeared to be the only guest awake. The dining buffet was set with an enormous coffeepot, mugs, and a large tray of freshly baked pastries covered with plastic wrap. Serving dishes lay empty awaiting breakfast entrées not yet prepared for the sleeping houseguests.

Suited in her white uniform and tall chef's hat, Lexie emerged from the kitchen. "Mr. Matt, may I cook you some breakfast now?"

"No thanks, Lexie. I'll eat with the others." She quietly disappeared into the kitchen. Matt poured a mug of coffee and lifted the plastic wrapper to sample a warm pastry.

Matt carefully balanced the coffee mug while devouring the scrumptious pastry and sauntered down the hall and into the library. He sat in front of the French doors and watched and listened as the wetlands stirred to wakefulness. "Life can't get any better than this," he thought momentarily. Then suddenly the appalling circumstances of the past few days resurfaced and a staggering sense of grief engulfed him again.

"Thought I smelled coffee," a gruff voice interrupted Matt's reflective mood. Matt turned to see Ignatius accompanied by his spirited canine companion. Pete although bouncing up and down was restrained, and Matt could not remember ever seeing the dog leashed in the house.

"What's with the leash, Ignatius?" Matt said as he stood up.

"Oh, Pete doesn't like the poop pad that Margot gave me to put on the bathroom floor. So, I put a leash on him and stuck him out the terrace door to go. He didn't like the rain either." As if affirming his master's comment, Pete shook vigorously.

"I'll get you a cup of coffee." Matt left and returned with a cup of coffee in one hand and a plate containing several pastries in the other. "Wait'll you taste these pastries."

Ignatius bit half a pastry. He rolled his eyes and gave a vigorous nod. "Yeah, I've got to have a talk with Lexie before we leave this place. That woman is one hell of a cook."

"Speaking of this place, Ignatius, I'm really sorry about our screwed up trip. I can't think of anything worse than this for a vacation."

"Oh, I don't know, Matt. I can think of something worse. How about an all expense paid vacation to a leprosy colony?" Matt's jaw dropped. Ignatius laughed. "Just kidding Matt. Hey these things happen. You had no control over your cousin's death nor the weather."

"Morning Matthew, 'Natius." Ben entered the library scratching his head vigorously and raking his fingers through his unruly hair in a half-hearted attempt to comb it. "Slept like a log. Give me rain on the roof and a little wind in the trees, and I sleep like a baby in my mama's arms. How about you guys? Sleep okay?"

Ignatius looked disgusted. "Can't say as I did, Ben. All that rumbling and snoring in the next room was enough to wake the dead."

"Oh, dear, don't say that," The men turned to see Peedee standing in the library doorway, her hand stretched wide upon her ample bosom. "Don't tempt the spirits, please. When the wind blows continuously as it did last night, we are at the mercy of any spirit that may be trapped between earth and heaven." Then she abruptly turned and walked toward the dining room.

"Shall we have breakfast now?" She called matter of factly over her shoulder.

Ignatius and Benjamin gaped at Matt.

"What was that all about?" Ignatius demanded.

Matt attempted to explain. "Aunt Peedee's a good old gal, but she has this thing about ghosts and spirits. She claims to have psychic impressions and some kind of cosmic connection. When we were kids she entertained us with all kinds of ghost stories. Uncle Will was always patient and simply claimed that embellishment is a southern gift and told us to indulge her. My parents shrugged her off, and Grandma Murray said we should over-look Peedee's little perculiars and focus on her virtues of which she has many. On the other hand, Wilson Delamar used Peedee's yarns to frighten Margot and Annie-Ann. He was a real worm back then—and still is."

"Well, Matt," scoffed Ignatius, "you've got quite a gene pool to choose from."

"Now hold on a minute, I've heard tell of lots of folks who have *the gift*," drawled Ben. "Don't go putting Matt's Aunt Peedee down like that, 'Natius "

"I hold such things in profound contempt," sneered Ignatius. "And frightening little girls …," he was interrupted as Steve walked into the room.

"Hey guys. Sorry I slept in. Carrie didn't sleep well with all the rain and wind whistling around this old house. This place is really like a tomb isn't it? I expected some spook to reach out from under the bed and grab my ankle."

"Now don't you go starting with the ghost stuff," warned Ben. ""Natius just had a hissy fit 'cause he found out that Peedee believes in spirits."

Steve laughed. "That's my Aunt Peedee. She aims to entertain."

Matt changed the subject. "It looks like the rain has let up for the time being. How would you guys feel about going out to where they found Noah? I know the spot. Even know the man who owns the property."

"You saying we're gonna do a little investigating?" Ben asked excitedly.

"Well, not a *real* investigation, but I'd like to get a better picture of what happened, and it helps to actually see the place. His body was found pretty close to the shore."

"Count me in," said Ben eagerly.

"Me, too. Since the rain's reduced to a drizzle, does this mean your hurricane's over?" asked Ignatius.

Matt laughed. "The hurricane hasn't got here yet. This rain and wind is just an introduction. The last report I heard said Hurricane Jean is just heading inland down in North Carolina."

Steve said, "Matt I don't think I'll go with you. I'll just hang here in case something comes up. Besides Carrie doesn't feel well. I'm not so sure we should have stayed here. It's got her upset."

Matt's voice showed concern. "Sure Steve. Would you rather we not go?"

"No, no. I'm anxious to get your take on things down there."

"Okay. After we eat then," Matt said, and he headed toward the smell of Smithfield ham, eggs, and buttermilk pancakes coming from the dining room.

As the men stepped into the hall, a maid approached Ben. "Mr. Day, you have a long distance phone call from Winchester, Tennessee. You may take it in the hall or in your room."

"Thanks, I'll take it here," said Ben. "You guys go head. I'll catch up with you."

Ignatius, Matt, and Steve joined Peedee in the dining room. The buffet was ladened with a grand breakfast fare. Silver serving platters held slices of Smithfield ham, strips of thick bacon, and sausage patties. Large covered bowls contained eggs, hash browns, corn beef hash, and grits. Baskets held brightly colored towels that covered hot buttermilk biscuits and toast. And, of course, there was the replenished platter filled with a variety of warm pastries.

Margot and Einer joined the group, and Ignatius looked around the table at the brimming plates. "You'd think we're a bunch of field hands getting ready for a hard day's work."

Matt laughed. "Ignatius, what does a guy from Colorado know about field hands?"

Ignatius did not have a chance to answer Matt's question. Ben entered the room shaking his head and laughing.

"Well, let's have it, Ben," said Ignatius. "What's so funny in Winchester?"

Ben went to the buffet and began to fill his plate. Grinning he said, "Matt, 'Natius, seems like we're suspects."

"What?" the diners said simultaneously. Einer's face took on a stern expression.

"Yep," said Ben taking his place at the table. "Seems like those officers who were here yesterday checked us out. Called the Winchester City Police Department and inquired about a suspicious looking character named Benjamin Day. The Winchester policeman spotted the opportunity to pull a good one on my secretary, so they referred the detective to Penny, over at the Franklin County Sheriff's Office. Said they remembered hearing her speak of a fugitive by the name of Day." Ben laughed and took a bite of ham savoring the wonderful flavor.

"Well, and what happened?" Ignatius demanded impatiently.

"What happened was that they called Penny. When she realized the prank the Winchester policemen played on her, she pitched a doozy and tore into everyone around. Poor old Dexter. He ain't come down off the ceiling yet." Ben shook his head and laughed. "Yes sir, those guys really got little Miss Penny's goat."

"Well, I don't take to practical jokes myself. Especially where police work is concerned," said Ignatius.

"Oh, lighten up, 'Natius," said Ben. "In law enforcement you have to let go sometimes. If you let things get too heavy, you'll crack up. Besides, that was Penny on the phone, and she's over it now. We had a good laugh."

But Einer Pellinger was not laughing.

* * *

The Chief sat rigidly behind his desk, his arms folded and a scowl on his face. He was obviously not pleased with Audrey and Donald's report. His probing eyes darted from Donald to Audrey. Donald averted his gaze, but Audrey eyed him squarely.

"Just where the hell are you going with this, Detective Kelly?" he finally demanded.

"What? I don't understand…"

"Listen up Kelly, Anderson…" He stood up and braced himself as he stretched his neck across the desk. "We got a murder here. A man not packing a full load goes around liberating crabs from watermen's pots. One day this man drowns. Not by accident but murder. Now is it too much of a stretch to conclude simply that some waterman got pissed off about losing their catch and decided to put an end to Noah's vandalism. So he caught Noah in the act of emptying a pot, strikes him with an unidentified object, and drowns him. End of problem." He tossed the pen with which he had been dallying upon his desk. "Now this seemed like a simple case to me so I'm thought that this would be a good one for two young officers to get some real investigative experience. And what do you do? You're off questioning the whole family, their doctor, even their out-of town guests."

Donald opened his mouth to explain but the Chief raised his palm to silence him. "Yeah, I know all about your phone call to Winchester, Tennessee to check on none other than the Sheriff of Franklin County Tennessee. This could turn ugly, Kelly, Anderson, real ugly."

"We were just working from the premise that with a murder you always start the investigation with the family," Audrey tried to explain.

"Always?" scoffed the Chief. "Always is too absolute, Kelly. Sometimes the simplest explanation is the right one."

Audrey and Donald looked crestfallen. Realizing that he may have come down too hard on the young detectives, the Chief sat down and softened his voice. "Look Detectives, what's wrong with this picture? Beautiful, five foot two, one hundred and ten pound Margot

Pellinger gets tired of baby sitting her six foot three, two hundred and eighty pound cousin. So she goes out at the crack of dawn, climbs into a boat all alone, follows him out to the crab pots, beats him with an oar and drowns him. She thinks this would be a better solution than asking her doting husband to use his money and connections to get rid of someone who had become a burden to her."

Donald asked, "How do we know that she didn't go with him in his boat?"

"You haven't even done your homework, Anderson. Think. They found Noah's boat on the bottom of the river close to the body. Someone had beaten holes in the bottom. And unless the perpetrator walked on water, he came in another boat. Besides that's not the point." He leaned forward on his desk. "You've gone too far afield...'

"What about Mr. Pellinger? We learned the other night that he does not like anyone upsetting Margot...uh Mrs. Pellinger. How angry would he have to get to take matters in his own hands?" Audrey tried to redeem herself.

"Do you really want to go down that slippery slope, Kelly?" The Chief paused to give emphasis to this cautionary question. Audrey, however, appeared to expect an answer. "Detective, you're talking about a man who has unlimited financial resources. The man has wheeled and dealed with the shrewdest men, not just in Virginia, but all over the country. If he wanted to get rid of Noah, he could find a more clever way to do it... a way that would cast absolutely no suspicion on his wife or him. No siree, if a successful man like Pellinger was responsible for this murder, you can be sure that no tracks would lead to Berryhill."

Audrey and Donald were abashed. Their first case, and according to the Chief, they were puffing down the wrong track.

After what seemed to be an interminable silence, the Chief said, "Now I'll tell you what to do. I want you to go on out there to the scene of the crime again and talk to everybody who knew Noah. Who knew he was releasing crabs, who knew the areas he frequented? Who was angry with him? Then come back here and let's see what you've got."

He reached for the telephone and punched a number. As he waited, receiver to his ear, he waved Audrey and Donald out of his office.

* * *

"Well, that was humiliating," said Donald as he steered the car onto John Tyler Highway. "I feel like some kid who just got tossed out of the principal's office. Guess we really got off to a lousy start."

"I don't know, Donald," said Audrey. "I agree that it's vital to interrogate the people at the scene. I was going to suggest that we do that this afternoon anyway. But I still think something doesn't float right with that family, and I think the Chief is trying to steer us in another direction because he doesn't want to deal with Pellinger's clout. "

"Oh, come on, Audrey. Let it go for heaven's sake. If we keep poking around at Berryhill, we're going to land behind some desk until we're old enough to retire."

Audrey appeared to be oblivious to Donald's resistance. She stared intently ahead and spoke almost as if she were talking to herself. "The Chief doesn't want us to officially investigate the people at Berryhill, but he couldn't object if we made a personal visit...say, to take flowers of condolence to our old classmate. We could..."

"We? We? Where do you get that comrade stuff? Listen, Audrey, anything that even remotely resembles breaking the Chief's orders, count me out!" Donald shouted.

Donald swung the vehicle onto a dirt road and they jounced the rest of the way to the bank of the James River. Audrey remained silent staring thoughtfully out of the window.

Chapter 11

Ignatius' van reeled as he navigated potholes and debris on the bumpy gravel road. As they emerged from the woods, the James River came into view. A battered wooden shack was situated on the bank of the river. The shack was surrounded by stacks of wire crab pots. An unshaven, slovenly dressed man about Matt's age sat on a bench fashioned from a long plank and two supporting boards. He was using nylon line to tie styrofoam buoys to the wire pots. He heard the crunching sound as the van drove onto crushed oyster shells that surfaced the parking lot, but he gave no obvious indication that he recognized its occupants and continued his work.

"This is some view," said Ignatius as he pulled into a handicapped parking spot facing the river. "I'll just sit here and enjoy it while you two see what you can find out." He reached for a fishing magazine and settled back to wait.

Matt and Ben climbed out of the van. Ben was captivated by the sight. "What a beautiful spot, Matthew. Bet you had a blast on this river when you were a kid."

Matt smiled. "You can say that again." He looked toward the shack at the bottom of the hill. "And I think I see someone who had a blast with me."

Matt trudged down the hill toward the shack. "Hey, Adam," he shouted. "It's Matt Murray. How you doing?"

The man looked up and a faint smile creased his lips. "I thought that was you, Matt," he replied laying the line and buoy on the ground. He stood and moved toward Matt, his grimy hand extended.

Matt grasped his hand firmly and gave it a vigorous shake. "It's been a long time Adam. You look like you're staying busy." Matt nodded toward the pile of crab pots.

Adam shrugged. "Same old, same old. Things don't change much for me."

At that point, Ben joined the two men at the bottom of the hill. "Adam Ricks, this is my friend Benjamin Day from Winchester, Tennessee. He's the sheriff back there." Then waving up to Ignatius, Matt said, "And that is my other friend Ignatius Harder. I promised them both a vacation in one of the most beautiful spots in the world, but so far, we've attended a funeral and watched weather reports of Hurricane Jean."

As he exchanged waves with Ignatius, Adam noticed that the van was parked in the handicap space. "Say, I'm sorry to hear about your cousin, Noah. He was all right. But I don't mind telling you he caused some of us crabbers a lot of grief."

"I can imagine," Matt empathized. "The whole family is sorry about that, Adam. Believe me it became a real embarrassment."

"It's not y'all's fault. Noah was right pitiful. I always felt real sorry for him. Besides, Mr. Pellinger talked to all of us about it. He reimbursed us for anything we lost and told us he was looking to find a companion for Noah to keep him out of trouble. Mr. Pellinger really felt responsible," Adam said.

Matt said, "Thanks for telling me that Adam. I feel lots better knowing that Noah wasn't hated."

"Well somebody hated him," declared Ben. "Hated him enough to beat him over the head and drown him."

"Did you know he was murdered, Adam?" Matt asked.

"Sure. Word travels fast about murder, you know. Especially if the victim is related to Einer Pellinger's wife. But I'll tell you one thing. I don't know of anyone who hated Noah enough to kill him." Adam answered. "Sheriff, you helping out with the investigation?"

"No," replied Ben. "Guess my curiosity is an occupational hazard. Tend to get all inquisitive when it comes to murder."

"You guys want to sit down?" Adam invited pointing to the plank benches. The three men moved toward the benches, and Adam cleared the seat of lines and buoys. They sat facing the river.

"I couldn't leave it, Matt." Adam said nodding his head toward the river. "Besides I wasn't like you. I wouldn't have been happy up in Charlottesville or any other place for that matter. This old brackish water's in my veins."

"Well, I got news for you. It's still in my veins, too," said Matt. "Adam, what can you tell me about the discovery of Noah's body?"

"Not much to tell," said Adam. "Did you know I was the one who found him?"

"No," said Matt. "I knew he'd been found close to your place, but I didn't know that you actually found him."

"Yes. You see, we went out to empty the crab pots that morning and…"

"'Cuse me, Adam. You said *we*. Who was with you…if you don't mind me asking," Ben asked apologetically.

Adam said, "My grandson, Joshua. Actually the pots belonged to him. As I was saying, we went out to empty the crab pots and when we got to his spot, we saw something floating just under the water. I didn't think nothing of it at first. Thought it was some kind of trash. Then when we got closer, I reached over with my hook and gave it a little push. It rolled over, and a face appeared. It was all swollen and everything. Oh, sorry, Matt. Didn't mean to be insensitive."

"That's okay. Go ahead, Adam," Matt said encouragingly.

"Like I said, his face was so swollen that I didn't even recognize him. I tell you we got out of there in a hurry. Came back here and call the police," Adam said simply.

"Got a phone here?" asked Ben.

"Cell phone."

Matt tried to be cautious. "I hope Joshua wasn't too upset with Noah for tampering with his crab pots."

As if reading his thoughts, a troubled look appeared on Adam's face. He quickly regained his composure and said, "Joshua knew that Mr. Pellinger was reimbursing for losses. He wouldn't have been mad at Noah." Then as an afterthought, Adam volunteered, "You know, Joshua just got back from Camp Chanco? He'd been there the whole week before Noah was found. I put out his pots for him while he was gone."

Matt felt embarrassed. "Joshua is lucky to have a grandpa like you, Adam," he said in an effort to defuse the situation.

The men sat quietly looking out on the river. Small white caps lapped the shoreline and the marsh grass waved as the wind increased. An osprey winged toward its nest on a river marker sounding a piercing bleep, as if delivering an omen of treacherous weather to its mate. Matt breathed deeply and resurrected thoughts of happier times in this picturesque setting. Then he thought of Noah's body bobbing about in the murky river for two days and two nights. He turned up his jacket collar in an effort to check the chill that suddenly gripped him.

Ben was first to break the silence. He mused, "I wonder 'xactly what the murder scene looks like. I've never had a case where the victim was discovered in the water."

Adam stirred. "Would you like to see the spot, Sheriff? That is if you don't mind being pitched about. The water's picking up out there," he said. Adam was excited at the possibility of accompanying a Sheriff to the scene of a crime...even if the sheriff had no authority in James City County.

Ben gave the impression that the suggestion surprised him. "Why Adam, I most certainly would. And I wouldn't mind being pitched about. Heck, I'm a seasoned fisherman. Been pitched about a lot in my life. What do you say, Matt, you up to going out there?"

Matt recalled another time when Ben pulled him into a murder investigation. He had sworn not to let Ben suck him into another one. But this was different. This was his cousin who had never harmed a thing in his life, not even a crab.

"Sure. Thanks, Adam. I'll go tell Ignatius what's up." Matt sprinted up the hill in the direction of the van.

After informing Ignatius of their plan, Matt joined the other two men just in time to hear Ben say "Chicken wire? Just plain old chicken wire?"

"Yeah, the crab pot's a wooden frame that I make myself and enclose with chicken wire. Costs me about twenty bucks a pot. See these four openings that's so the crabs can get in to eat the bait."

"What you use for bait?" Ben asked always the avid fisherman.

"Oh, I use fish parts, eel, chicken necks…that kind of stuff. When the crab can't get out the same way he got in, he floats up here," said Adam pointing to an inner wire section of the pot. Then he's trapped and you got yourself a crab."

Adam looked up as Matt joined them. "Ready to go?" he asked.

Adam placed a ten horse power outboard motor and a boat hook into the boat. Then the three men drug the flat bottom boat down to the riverbank and eased it into the water. After wading out a few feet, they attached the outboard and climbed into the boat. White caps cast the little boat about forcefully, as Adam fired the motor and headed out onto the river.

"The spot's a little way down the river, Ben," Adam shouted over the din of the motor. "I try to find a place that don't get too much boat traffic, 'cause you never set a pot down in a boat channel. Boaters hate picking their way through a minefield of crab pots. With this boat, I can get in real shallow water. Don't have to worry about plowing down in the mud with a flat bottom. Shallow water is especially best in May and June. That's when the crabs come to rub themselves off."

"Rub themselves off?" asked Ben.

"Yeah, that's when they shed their shells and hide from the fish on the bottom," explained Adam.

Adam turned his boat starboard toward a cove set respectfully away from the river channel. "Check your pots every day?" asked Matt.

"Try to," answered Adam. "If the weather is too bad I can skip a day, but crabs are carnivores. If they stay shut up too long without food, they'll start to eat each other. So I try to empty the pot every day."

"Adam, had you checked your pots the day before the authorities say Noah died?" asked Ben.

Adam hesitated, a thoughtful look on his face. "Now let me see," he thought. "Come to think of it, I don't think I did, Ben. Do you think that means anything, Sheriff?" he asked excitedly.

Ben smiled, "I don't know, Adam, but all information is considered important in a murder investigation."

Matt marveled at Ben's ability to use ordinary people as sleuths. Adam killed the engine and the boat drifted slowly into a cove. The water was shallow, and marsh grass grew along the shoreline. As the boat bobbed about, Adam lifted his boat hook and pointed, "Over there, Ben," said Adam. "I believe the body was right about there. Of course, I could be a little off. Hard to be exact on water you know."

Matt and Ben stared at the spot where Noah's body was found. A small water snake resented the intrusion and slithered off through the marsh grass. Matt shivered.

"You okay, Buddy?" asked Ben.

"Yeah," Matt replied. His throat was dry.

"Shoreline's pretty close here. Adam, that looks like a footpath going up that embankment there," said Ben pointing to a path almost hidden by undergrowth. "Where does it go?"

"That goes up to a little back road that eventually comes out on John Tyler Highway," said Adam.

"Well, I guess the murderer could have left the scene by land or water," Ben stated simply.

The wind grew and swayed the boat reminding the men of the approaching storm. "Guess we'd better head on back," said Adam. He pulled the rope on the motor to fire it, and pointed the boat out into the river again. They moved faster and with more urgency as they headed back to the fishing shack.

"Do you always drop your pot in that same spot, Adam?" shouted Matt above the roar of the motor.

"Not all the time, but I try to put my pots in as safe a place as possible. If a boat severs my pot from its buoy, it cost me money. Not only do I lose my catch, I also lose my pot."

As they turned into Adam's cove, the men saw two uniformed officers sitting on the bench eyes staring intently in their direction.

Matt said, "Wonder what they want?"

Adam groaned, and Ben grinned widely when he recognized Audrey.

* * *

Earlier when the officers drove into the parking lot above Adam Rick's fishing shack, Donald parked between a Jeep and a battered old Crown Victoria Ford. The two vehicles suggested that the owners were determined fishermen who refused to be deterred by the forecast of an approaching hurricane. However, the vehicle that attracted the attention of the detectives was parked in a handicap parking space. It was a specially equipped, red van displaying a Tennessee license plate.

"Well, what do you know, Audrey? Mr. Ricks's got himself some out-of-town company," Donald said.

"Damn," Audrey swore. "Now what do you think they're doing here? We're supposed to conduct an investigation with them under foot?"

"Look out there." Donald pointed to a small boat being tossed about by white caps and an increasing wind. The boat held three occupants, and it was headed towards the crime scene. "What do you think we ought to do?"

"I don't know. I certainly don't feel like sitting here twiddling my thumbs while we wait for those three to get back from their boat ride." Audrey looked in the direction of the van. "Why don't we talk to him?" She nodded towards Ignatius just as he glanced up from his magazine.

Donald groaned. "Wouldn't that be going against the Chief's orders?"

"I don't know, Donald," Audrey replied irritably opening the door. "We could go back and ask him."

The two detectives approached the van. Audrey tapped on the window and signaled for Ignatius to lower it. A scowling Ignatius looked up from magazine and lowered the window.

"Mr. Harder? If I remember correctly," Audrey said.

"You remember correctly," huffed Ignatius.

"Didn't expect to see you here." Audrey said. Ignatius said nothing.

"May I ask what you are doing here?" Audrey continued.

"No."

"Is there some reason why you won't tell me why you're here?"

"Is there some reason why you're asking?"

Donald became apprehensive at the tone of this conversation. He cleared his throat and nudged Audrey's foot with his shoe.

Audrey backed off. "Well, I hope we didn't disturb you Mr. Harder. We're just trying to investigate this murder, and we aim to be thorough."

"Huh," grunted Ignatius, and he closed the window and resumed his reading.

Donald and Audrey walked down the hill to the shack and sat on the benches to wait.

"Audrey, we aren't supposed to be questioning the family, remember? We're here to talk to the guy who found the body," Donald reminded her.

"Yeah, yeah."

The detectives watched impatiently as the size of the white caps grew concurrently with the increase in the wind. A fishing boat occupied by two sulking fishermen appeared who had been forced to abandon their fishing plans. Reluctantly they tied up their boat and left with empty coolers they'd hope to fill with fish. They nodded to the detectives and prodded up the hill to the parking lot. Finally the boat carrying the three men appeared in the cove and headed to shore. As the bottom of the boat scraped the muddy river bottom, Adam jumped out and began to pull it ashore. Matt nodded a greeting to the two detectives. Ben flashed a big grin, and it was directed straight at Audrey. No reaction.

When the boat was on shore, Audrey spoke directly to Adam as if Matt and Ben were not there. She was determined not to be snubbed again. "Mr. Ricks, we're Detectives Kelly and Anderson. We talked with you earlier in the investigation. We would like to ask you some follow-up questions."

"Yes, I remember you. What kind of questions?" asked Adam.

"If you've got a minute, please, Mr. Ricks," added Donald.

"I want to get this boat away from the water before the storm gets here. Wind's already picking up. Then I'll be glad to talk to you. I don't know of anything to add to what I already said though." He began to drag the boat across the sand and away from the water.

"Wait a minute Adam," said Matt. "I'll give you a hand." He got behind the boat and pushed it toward the fishing shack.

Ben did not offer to help, and his wry smile remained fixed on Audrey. "How's the investigation going, Detectives?" he asked jovially. Neither Audrey nor Donald replied.

"A real shame about Noah Murray. Sounds like he was a real fine fellow. Makes it 'specially hard if the victim's a real nice fellow. Don't you think?" He persisted still grinning.

"I'm sorry, Mr. Day, we're not at liberty to discuss the case while it's still under investigation," said Audrey.

Ben's smile widened. "Don't you want to ask *me* some question? Be glad to help in any way I can. This seems to be the only game in town..."

Audrey snapped. "What makes you think we'd want your help?"

"Well, somebody does. Somebody called my secretary back in Winchester, Tennessee 'bout a possible suspect named Benjamin Day." Ben was finding it difficult to contain his laughter.

Audrey was incensed. She turned to Ben, eyes flashing. "Mr. Day, why do you think I would want to ask *you* questions...or even talk to you? Do you really think we need your help in this investigation? So what if someone is calling your secretary and asking about you. Do you think I know anyone interested in you?"

"Whoa there, Miz. Kelly..."

"*Detective* Kelly."

"Sorry, Detective Kelly. I didn't mean to rile you. But it seems to me like you're beating around the bush. And I might as well warn you, I'm a bush whacker." Ben suddenly exploded with a big guffaw. Donald, who had chosen to be a silent bystander during the exchange, burst into laughter too. Audrey shot him a disgusted look and stomped towards the fishing shack.

"She doesn't mean anything by it, Sheriff Day. She just gets impressed with herself. She's really one smart woman," Donald said in defense of his partner.

"That she is Donald. And she's one good looking woman too." Ben added with a wink.

Matt did not speak as he and Ben climbed to the parking lot. Ben respected his silence for a few minutes and then said, "You okay, buddy?"

106

"I suppose so, Ben. It's hard enough to believe Noah is dead. But it's wrenching to think of the brutal way he died and to know he was in that river for two days and two nights. I couldn't wait to get out of that boat."

"Had a feeling you shouldn't have gone out there," Ben said laying a hand on Matt's shoulder.

They climbed into the van and Ignatius readied himself for the report. "How was it?" he asked.

"Rough," replied Matt.

Matt and Ben recounted how Adam found Noah's body and described the site of the murder. Ignatius listened silently. When they completed their account Ignatius said, "Those two officers who called Winchester to check on us as suspects tried to question me."

"And?" prompted Matt.

"I didn't have time for them," he scoffed.

"Now, 'Natius, they was use trying to do their job," Ben mused.

"Yeah, Ben had time for them," snickered Matt, "especially for the attractive woman cop. Didn't you, Ben?"

"Now that's between me and her," said Ben. He folded his arms and flashed a broad smile. Then he pulled his hat over his eyes and slid down into his seat.

"Oh geez," Ignatius groaned as he rolled his eyes and steered the van toward Berryhill.

Chapter 12

On the first night of their stay at Berryhill, Carrie and Margot checked on Peedee before turning in. Peedee seized their visit as an opportunity to render an uncanny performance for them. She began with a tearful episode, and then consoled herself by expounding on her views of life after death.

"We should not grieve for Noah you know," Peedee sniffed. "Death is not to be feared. Death is simply life after life. Sometimes those who have passed don't understand what has happened and refuse to go on to the next life. They become earthbound. Those are the restless spirits, or ghosts, as we sometimes call them. I fear that poor Noah doesn't understand what has happened to him. That's why I feel his presence so strongly."

Margot, who was accustomed to Peedee's ramblings, appeared blase. Carrie, on the other hand, had been frightened. She shuddered as the wind whistled through the trees and rattled the windows producing eerie sounds.

When Carrie returned to her room, Steve was sleeping peacefully, his face hidden in a soft eider down pillow. Carrie roused Steve and told him of Peedee's dramatic performance. She also told him of her fear...fear fed by Peedee's inane insistence that spirits were present in the house, and that she served as a conduit for their manifestations. Steve dismissed Peedee's prattle as superstitious tripe, turned over, and promptly fell asleep again.

Carrie, however, slept fitfully and awakened early. She was exhausted, and her head hurt. First light penetrated the sheer window covering, and outside the bedroom window aged limbs of the gigantic oaks waved their early morning greeting. As time passed, Carrie found their motion to be soothing and non-threatening. The rain had subsided again, and there was little evidence of the hurricane that was presently assaulting inland North Carolina.

Carrie quietly slipped from bed and made her way to a large over-stuffed chair positioned by the window. The view from this station was perfect for early morning reveries. A spectacular view of the James River could be seen through the fluttering green leaves. Small patches of mist that had not yet dissipated swirled aimlessly above the marsh grass in an attempt to escape the vaporizing sunlight. Silhouettes of water birds winged against the red sky as they began their morning foraging, and a black-hooded laughing gull complained to anything that would listen. A splash erupted as a fish leaped and snared a dragonfly that hovered carelessly close to the water. Small waves lapped the riverbank and a sandpiper pursued the retreating water hopeful that some delicacy might have been uncovered.

On the river, a brave wind surfer outfitted in a wet suit stood confidently on his board. His sail was full, and the fluky gusts presented quite a challenge. He was obviously skilled, and he engaged the wind in breath-taking and exhilarating feats. Carrie watched him tack back and forth hiking out if the wind threatened to topple him. He worked the board farther and farther out into the river. Then as the craft silhouetted the rosy horizon, Carrie watched its sail changed from white to red. A foreboding memory came to her. Steve's grandmother often recited an old nautical adage, "Red sails at night, sailor's delight. Red sails in the morning, sailors take warning."

Carrie suddenly darted across the room and shook Steve vigorously. "Steve, wake up. Get up. I want to leave right now."

It had not been easy for Steve to convince Carrie to remain at Berryhill. He did not tell her how foolish it was to let Peedee upset her. Instead he used a pragmatic approach, arguing that this was no time to drive through the Hampton Roads Bridge/ Tunnel and back into Portsmouth. Flooding in low-lying areas was already being reported. As much as he loved Aunt Peedee, Steve was annoyed that she chose this time to give one of her *haunting* performances.

Steve persuaded Carrie to take a long soak in the tub and relax. He brought her tea and turned the radio to an oldies station. Then he joined the others for breakfast. Later, Steve would be glad he stayed behind while Matt and his friends drove to the murder site. There might truly have been a calamity had Einer been the only man at Berryhill when the next visitors arrived.

* * *

Margot and Carrie convinced Peedee that this morning would be a good time to write thank you notes for the many expressions of sympathy the family received following Noah's death. Armed with notes, cards, and address book, the three women staked out a work place on the large game table in the library. Any attempt by Peedee

110

to stray from the task at hand was quickly checked by Margot and Carrie, especially if the attempt took a supernatural turn.

Steve used the morning to fasten shutters on the three floors of Berryhill in preparation for the hurricane that was rapidly approaching the peninsula. He discovered that hinges on some of the shutters were rusted and this made securing them no easy task.

Einer did not go to his office this morning, instead, he chose to work at home. He quietly watched as Margo worked with Carrie and Peedee. Peedee's obsession with the paranormal was worrisome to Einer, but it did not appear to trouble Margot. With the exception of Carrie, the whole family viewed Peedee's eccentricities as her *usual* behavior.

The dark circles under Margot's eyes and the restless way she tossed at night concerned Einer. She seemed to draw strength from her cousins, but Einer feared this strength might be short-lived. He worried that when her cousins left she might collapse from the customary stresses that follow the death of a family member.

As if validating Einer's concern, a car horn blew a signature sequence announcing the arrival of one who thought very highly of himself.

Margot looked helplessly at Einer. "That's Daddy," she confirmed as if there were some doubt.

"Holy crap…"

"Einer Pellinnger!" admonished Margot. Einer stood and walked straight to the bar.

Margot walked toward him as if seeking protection. They stood facing the hallway. No door chime announced the visitors. Instead, the front door opened and a shrill female voice announced loudly, "Margot darling, it's Dorothy and Wilson."

A fastidiously dressed woman accompanied by an equally well-dressed man sailed into the room without invitation. The bodacious man had a luxurious tan and sported a pair of Oakley sunglasses propped upon his head in case the hurricane changed course and the sun suddenly bounced out. The woman wore perfectly- applied makeup, and her over-bleached hair was so heavily sprayed that she appeared to be wearing a helmet. They wore matching outfits…white deck shoes, white canvas slacks, and olive-green cashmere sweaters.

"Ken and Barbie," muttered Carrie.

"What was that, dear?" asked Peedee, a confused look on her face.

"Never mind," said Carrie.

"Margot, darling," gushed Dorothy as she rushed to brush a kiss on Margot's cheek.

"How's my girl?" asked Wilson his eyes never leaving Einer.

"I didn't expect you this morning," said Margot weakly. "We…Carrie and I are helping Aunt Peedee write thank-you notes."

"And we wouldn't dream of interrupting. Now come on over here and get right back to work." Dorothy steered Margot toward the game table and sat down. "Hello, Peedee, I hope you're feeling more rested today." She did not acknowledge Carrie. In Dorothy's opinion, Carrie did not warrant acknowledgement.

Wilson said, "Well, I see you've got company. After all the activities of the past few days, must be a pain in the ass to have to entertain."

112

"We're not *entertaining*, Wilson. Carrie is here because Margot wanted her. She is most certainly welcome," Einer said impatiently.

"Yes, and we know that Margot always gets what she want, don't we?" laughed Wilson. Einer looked irate. "Only kidding, Einer. I really appreciate your taking care of my little girl. You know she's the only child I have left." His face took on an exaggerated look of sadness.

Although Dorothy was seated with the other women, her ear was attuned to the conversation between Einer and Wilson. Wilson leaned closer to Einer. "Wonder if I might have a word with you in private, Einer?"

Einer looked disgusted and poured himself another drink. He did not offer Wilson a drink. After taking a hefty swallow, Einer slammed the glass on the bar and said, "Let's go across the hall."

The two men left the library and entered the parlor. Einer did not close the door, and although the conversation was muddled the tone was highly charged. Einer was obviously angry, and Wilson's persistence only served to kindle his ire. Dorothy ignored the women who were busily writing notes and strained unsuccessfully to decipher the words.

As the intensity of the men's voices increased, Margot and Carrie feigned a conversation to mask the argument across the hall.

"So…," Carrie said, "I told Steve that I think we should take advantage of this break in the rain to drive back to Portsmouth…"

Still straining to eavesdrop, Dorothy silenced Carrie by reaching across the table and patting her hand. "Yes, yes dear. I agree. This would be a good time for you and Steve to drive back. Now how about a stamp on this," she said as she flipped an envelop towards Carrie.

Just as the two men's voices reached a crescendo, Steve descended the stairs, "Hey, Wilson. I didn't know you were here."

Wilson glared at Steve and stormed out of the parlor, a look of rage on his face. "Let's go," he called going directly to the door. Dorothy leapt from the chair and like an automaton moved wordlessly behind her husband.

Wilson further demonstrated his rage by spraying a wake of gravel as he sped off in his silver Mercedes. His car veered sharply to the left. As Wilson struggled to regain control of his vehicle, he swerved again just in time to miss a red van turning onto the Berryhill coach road.

The occupants of the van gasped, and the driver swore, "What the hell…?"

"Ignatius, Ben, we just missed my Aunt Dorothy and her worthless husband, Wilson," said Matt sarcastically.

The silver Mercedes headed toward John Tyler Highway and disappeared.

When Ben, Ignatius, and Matt came into the house, they saw Steve and Einer, heads together in the parlor. Carrie, Margot and Aunt Peedee were in the library their attention focused on piles of cards and letters. Ben and Ignatius tactfully joined the women, but Matt headed for the parlor.

"What's going on?" asked Matt. "Wilson just about ran us off the road. Damn fool. If it hadn't been for Ignatius' driving…."

"Damn," said Einer. "Everything that man does is reckless. Was anyone hurt, Matt?"

"No, we're just fine. But he sure acted crazy. What?"

"Money. What else," replied Einer. "The man's a fool. One might think he's an abysmal failure, but he's never *attempted* anything, so how could he fail. The only reason in the world I ever helped him in the first place was because he's Margot's father. But when I started backing off, he reminded me one too many times that he's my wife's father. He tried to make me feel that I owe him something for marrying his daughter. It disgusted me that he would treat her like property. I kept hoping he'd change for the better, but people like Delamar never change. I told him the last time I bailed him out that there would be no other time. He apparently didn't believe me. I'll bet be believes me now."

"How will Margot feel about this?" asked Matt.

"Margot is in full agreement. We've talked about this at length. Her relationship with Wilson and Dorothy is not good anyway. Actually I think she feels liberated by my stand."

"Einer?" The three men turned to see Margot standing in the doorway.

Einer moved toward her, "It's alright, dear. Everything is alright." Matt and Steve walked to the library.

* * *

"Who the hell?" shouted Wilson as his car skidded barely missing the red van.

115

He did not stop when he reached John Tyler Highway but swerved abruptly onto the main road barely avoiding being hit by a sixteen wheeler. The truck driver laid on the horn and flipped Wilson a gesture as he fishtailed in an effort to bring the Mercedes under control.

Dorothy screamed and shoved her foot onto the floorboard in an effort to apply imaginary brakes. "You damned idiot! You want to kill us? If you're going to be such a fool, just pull over and let me drive. You hear me?"

Wilson calmed down. There was nothing more humiliating to him than being driven about by his wife. He slowed down and pounded his fist on the steering wheel. "Damn him. That arrogant... It's not as if he'd miss the money. Nobody ever told him that charity begins at home? I read in the Gazette about the money he gives to charity. Yet he won't even help his wife's father out of a jam. The bastard!"

Dorothy smoothed her clothes and patted her hair. "I take it then that he said no. So what are you going to do now Wilson? Huh?" she taunted.

Without giving a turn signal, Wilson veered left onto an unpaved road that led to the Delamar estate. Soon the car skidded to a halt in front of their home. The lack of care to the old mansion was immediately apparent. Loose bricks, missing mortar, and cracking paint made evident the need for maintenance. Although tidy, the yard needed care. Scrubs that had grown too tall needed pruning. Old oak trees hung on to dead limbs that threatened to crash onto the roof of the house. The lawn was more weeds than grass, and there were a generous number of bare spots dotting the yard.

Dorothy flipped her seat belt and was up the steps before Wilson had a chance to kill the engine. She banged the door and stomped into the parlor. She began to pace. She turned quickly as she heard the front door slam shut.

"So what now?" she cried angrily.

Wilson ignored the question. He was still furious with Einer. "He can play gracious host to Steve and what's her name…Carrie. But he can't be generous to his own wife's father. I'll say it again, charity begins at home."

"Well you don't have to worry about Steve and Carrie. They are taking advantage of the lull in the rain to go back to Portsmouth today. What you have to worry about is our situation. You've got to think of something. I'm fed up Wilson. Fed up with always having to buy on sale. Fed up with no help in keeping up this drafty old place. Fed up with being embarrassed because our club membership is past due. Fed up because our credit cards are maxed out, and we can't go out to eat. And fed up that I have a daughter who has everything I ever wanted. And do you know what else?" She was shouting. "She didn't have to turn a damned hand to get it. He just fell in her lap. Like a love-sick little puppy dog. He makes me sick! Sick I tell you! And what can you do? Nothing. *You* can't do a damned thing."

"Now, Dot…."

"And don't cal me *Dot*. My name is Dorothy. *Dot,* like I'm some damned little speck, although that's about all the consideration I ever get around here." She paused breathlessly and glared at him. "Maybe I need to take matters into my own hands."

Dorothy turned on her heel and stormed out of the room leaving a shattered Wilson in her wake.

117

* * *

Audrey and Donald felt discouraged as they returned to the station. They had learned nothing new from Adam Ricks. Their mood mimicked the weather that was deteriorating fast.

"Okay," said Donald. "No new leads there. Where do we go from here?'

"I don't know. Maybe we could ask the Chief," Audrey muttered as she sat down and absentmindedly shuffled through a stack of mail. She stopped as one letter caught her eye. The envelope was addressed to the attention of Detectives Kelly and Anderson and written in a childish block print. "Whoa, Donald, what have we got here?"

Donald moved to the desk as Audrey extracted a pair of latex gloves. She slipped them on, and using a sharp letter opener she carefully slid the blade along the sealed edge. Gently reaching inside she unfolded a one-page note. It was written in the same childish block print.

Donald, who was not wearing gloves said anxiously, "What does it say?"

Audrey read the note aloud:

DETECTIVES KELLY AND ANDERSON...YOU HAVE BEEN TRYING TO FIND OUT WHO WAS NOAH MURRAY'S REAL MOTHER. WHY DON'T YOU ASK HIS REAL FATHER, EINER PELLINGER?
      SOMEONE WHO WANTS TO HELP

118

Audrey and Donald stared at the note. Was this real or a joke played by some warped person?

"Just think, a few minutes ago we didn't have anything new to show the Chief," said Donald.

Audrey folded the letter carefully and slipped it back into the envelope. Smiling broadly she said, "Well, Donald, we certainly have something to show him now."

Chapter 13

Audrey and Donald knocked on the Chief's door. In response to a gruff "What?" they entered the office armed with their newly acquired evidence. Neither the Chief nor the Detectives spoke. Audrey simply passed the letter across the desk.

"You may want to use gloves, sir," suggested Donald.

The Chief reluctantly opened a desk drawer and retrieved a pair of latex gloves. "What is this?" he asked simply. He cautiously removed the letter from the envelope and read it. "Hell's bells," he gasped. "When did this come?"

"While we were out questioning Adam Ricks. By the way, no new information there," said Audrey.

"What's your take?" the Chief asked.

Audrey and Donald crossed behind the desk and leaned over the Chief's shoulder scrutinizing the letter more closely. The three studied it intently. The postmark was local, and the letter was mailed yesterday. The stamp was adhesive, not the lick type. The paper was white with blue lines, and there were particles of mucilage across the top. The sheet appeared to have been torn from a tablet, and was folded twice. The envelope was a small letter size, the kind that can be easily purchased at any drugstore or discount store. The childish block printing had been done with a blue ball point pen.

"No help from the envelope and paper. You can buy them from a hundred places," Donald said.

"Yeah," said Audrey. "And no DNA from the stamp. We need to dust for prints, but I'm betting we don't find any help there."

"What do you make of the writing?" asked Donald.

"My guess is someone used the hand they're not accustomed to writing with. Add exaggeration in size and style, makes it next to impossible to identify," Audrey muttered.

"Send it to the lab for prints and evaluation," said the Chief. "I agree, though. I don't think we'll find anything."

He motioned for the detectives to pull up chairs. "Would either of you like to take a swing at this?" he leaned forward, elbows on his desk.

"Well, sir, I think this casts suspicion on Einer Pellinger," Donald ventured hesitatingly. "He obviously doesn't want this known." He knew this sounded weak.

"Humm," said the Chief. "Kelly?"

"Well, this certainly does open up a whole new field of investigation," she began. "I think we definitely have to determine the credibility of this information. But, the thing that baffles me is, even if Pellinger is Noah's father, why would he murder him? It doesn't make sense. It is highly unlikely that Noah knew who his father was and besides no one would believe him if he told it." The Chief nodded his head in agreement.

"Also," Audrey continued, "if Pellinger wanted to get rid of Noah, why wait almost 40 years to do it?"

"Then you're saying you don't think Pellinger killed him?" asked Donald.

"No, I'm not saying that," Audrey said. "I'm just saying that simply finding out that Einer Pellinger is his father, doesn't give him a convincing motive."

"I agree," said the Chief.

"Why don't we check DNA?" suggested Donald.

"We can run one on Noah, but the trick will be to get Einer to agree to give a sample. If he concealed this for 40 years, he's not likely to go easy to be tested now," the Chief said.

The Chief stood and walked to the window. It was raining again. Soon all of the County's manpower would be utilized to deal with the emergencies resulting from Hurricane Jean. It would be frustrating to put this investigation on the back burner for even a day much less the weeks it might take for things to return to normal after the storm.

He turned toward the detectives, and said, "Okay, let's look at it like this. Why would someone want us to know that Einer Pellinger is Noah's father...if he actually is?"

"Good point, Chief," said Audrey.

"Also, who might *know* Einer is the father?" added Donald.

"Right. Now you're cooking, Anderson." The Chief seemed invigorated. "Did you two hear anything from his doctor or from his school that would lead you to believe that they might know who Noah's father is?"

Audrey smiled. She felt vindicated that the Chief now felt they had not wasted their time with the morning interviews. "No sir. Neither Dr. Harris nor Ms. Simms knew who his birth parents are."

"What about birth records?"

"We'll give it a try. We need to check the parents' names on the birth certificate. We don't know for certain when his birth date is. All we know is what the family told us. We aren't even certain he was born in Virginia. All we know is that Einer just handed a baby over to this old couple to care for. Hell that should have tipped us off."

"Okay," the Chief said, rubbing his hands together. "Here's where we go from here. First, check records that may indicate if Einer Pellinger is the father. Don't think it'll show anything, but check anyway. Next, you're gonna have to go back out to Berryhill and confront Einer Pellinger with this letter."

Audrey and Donald looked at each other with dread.

"You can be diplomatic. Tell him you received the letter and want to give him an opportunity to respond. After you hear what he has to say, bring up the DNA. But that's where you've got to be careful. At this point, we can't require him to co-operate--hell, I'm not sure we'll ever be able to *require* him to do anything. Questions?"

Audrey and Donald shook their heads.

"Okay, now get out of here. See how much you can do before that hurricane hits."

* * *

Lunch at Berryhill consisted of Hatteras style clam chowder, a mixed green salad, thin slices of cold Smithfield ham, hot White House rolls, and a cheese soufflé so light that it might have floated off the plate. Dessert was peach melba, a scoop of soft homemade vanilla ice cream covered with fresh peaches and topped with raspberry sauce. As usual, Ignatius took notice of the menu, especially the chowder.

Little conversation took place during the meal. And Einer cast a watchful eye on Margot who merely toyed with her food. After lunch it was suggested that they watch the latest report on Hurricane Jean. And it was not good.

Earlier that morning the hurricane roared inland, and Eastern North Carolina was slammed hard. It was already being termed a disaster area. An enormous amount of rain was dumped on an area where the soil was already completely saturated from days of rain. Shocking pictures appeared on the screen. People awaited rescue from rooftops as rushing water gushed from creek beds and swollen riverbanks. Farmers and local fishermen lifted babies and old people into their small powerboats. The bloated carcasses of cattle and hogs impeded their efforts. Dogs and cats struggled to stay afloat. Chickens clung to tree branches. Sludge from pig and chicken farms contaminated the water making it unusable.

Exhausted flood victims huddled in schools buildings and fire stations and comforted their crying children. Some victims played cards, and others whispered softly of the horrors they'd witnessed. Cots and sleeping bags were provided for the weary, and hopeful faces looked beseechingly into the lens of intruding television cameras. A weary Governor proclaimed the courage and determination of Eastern North Carolinians while appealing for assistance from any source.

The Norfolk television station flashed a map of eastern North Carolina showing the hurricane's path of destruction. It also predicted the continuing direction of Hurricane Jean. It would move across the Virginia state line and onto the peninsula later tonight. The storm would continue well into tomorrow. It was predicted that the greatest destruction would result from heavy rain falling upon an area where rivers and streams were already swollen and the ground completely saturated.

The viewers at Berryhill watched the destruction in horror. The ring of the telephone was almost lost in the drama of the suffering depicted on the television screen. The maid entered the library and interrupted by announcing that Margot had a telephone call. Margot shot Einer a look of dread. He said, "I'll get it, dear."

"No, Einer. I must learn to deal with Dot and Wilson. I can't always expect you to intercede."

Matt thought this was pretty gutsy of his cousin and was really proud of her. He wondered if being surrounded by family gave her confidence to confront them. A look at Einer showed him that her husband was also pleased. Einer winked at Matt.

Margot returned shortly, a wide grin upon her face. Einer said, "Well, dear?"

"It's okay, Einer. Matt," she said with a coy look upon her face, "there's someone who would like to speak with you."

"Me?" Matt thought of his sons in Tennessee. "Is anything wrong?" he asked. Not waiting for an answer Matt rose quickly and started to the hall.

"Hello," he said anxiously.

"Matt?" whispered a soft voice tinged with a slight tidewater accent and etched with concern. "Are you alright?"

Caryn? Oh, God, Caryn. Memories tenderly tucked away for many years surfaced. Conflicting memories. Memories of Caryn. Caryn who could be as sensual as a midnight swim in the ocean, or as pristine as the moonlight on the water. She could be as strong as the wind that fills the sails of a boat on the bay, or as gentle as a morning breeze. She could be as warm as the taste of good brandy, or as cool as sweet iced tea. She could be loquacious or pensive, flamboyant or reserved, and she was a part of Matt's past here in James City County so many years ago.

"Caryn, what an unexpected surprise." Matt's voice was hoarse. "Are you in Williamsburg?"

"No. I just learned of Noah's death. I called to convey my condolences to Margot. I didn't know you were there." Caryn explained. "My condolences to you also, Matt. I know you all loved Noah."

"Thank you, Caryn. Noah was special in so many ways. In spite of the problems that arose the last few months, he'll be greatly missed."

"Problems? What problems, Matt?"

Matt explained Noah's obsession with wildlife, especially crabs, and the problems he'd caused the watermen. "Now we are told that Noah was murdered. Did Margot tell you that?"

"No, Margot didn't tell me, but I'd heard it from a friend who called to tell me of Noah's death. Matt, this makes his death even more tragic."

"Yes, it does. Ben, Ignatius, and I went out to the site of the murder today. This is going to be a hard one to solve, I'm afraid."

"Ben? Ignatius? Are they with you?"

"Yes, we came here for a vacation, but it's turned into the vacation from hell."

"Does this mean the Terrific Tennessee Trio is embarking upon yet another murder investigation?" Caryn teased.

Matt said. "No, I just had to see the site of his death for myself…and you remember Ben. Well, he was anxious to take a look."

"Oh yes, I recall Ben." There was a long awkward pause. Finally Caryn said, "How long will you be in James City County?"

"Haven't decided. Of course, a lot depends upon the weather."

"Well, when the hurricane passes I may come down for a visit…if you're still there."

"That would be great, Caryn," murmured Matt. "Hope to see you then."

"Me, too. So long Matt."

"So long." Matt was excited but wary. He felt less vulnerable when Caryn was just a memory.

* * *

"Margot, do you know who was on the phone?" asked Ignatius concern evident in his voice. "No problem with Matt's sons, I hope."

Margot smiled. "Oh, don't worry, Ignatius. There's nothing wrong. In fact, there could be something very right. That was Caryn. Caryn Shipley."

"Now Margot, be careful. It can be dangerous playing matchmaker," Einer warned.

"I know, Einer," said Margot. "But I can't help thinking how wonderful it would be if after all these years Matt and Caryn could get back together."

Einer rolled his eyes and sighed.

"Margot," said Ben. "You know, I've spoken with Caryn on the telephone in regard to a case I had in Tennessee, and I've heard Matt speak of her. And I've always felt there was more to it than just a casual relationship. Am I wrong or what?"

Margot was excited. She spoke rapidly and in lowered voice. "No, Ben you're absolutely right. There's always been a kind of connection between them. Even when they were very young, they were always together…biking, swimming, hiking. Later they were confidants and always defended each other. One seemed to know what the other was thinking even before they spoke. They dated in high school, but their relationship still remained on just a friendship basis. Neither of them seemed to want to be the one to take things to the next level. Then…" Margot paused and rubbed her hands together, delighting in the resurgence of memories from more innocent times. "Then enters Hank."

"Hank?" said Ignatius and Ben in unison.

"Yes, Hank," continued Margot. "Hank was soooo handsome, sooo smooth, sooo much of a know-it all. But Caryn fell for him. I think it crushed Matt, but he let it happen. He just accepted Hank and refused to defend his relationship with Caryn."

"Margot," said Steve, "you're forgetting that there wasn't really a relationship there…not one like you're thinking. I tried to get Matt to tell Caryn how he felt about her. I tired. But he was just so damned afraid of appearing foolish. He wouldn't tell her how he felt. You can't blame Caryn for getting impatient."

"You're right Steve. I just always hoped that somehow they'd get together," said Margot.

"Well, what about Jill?" said Ignatius. He seemed troubled by what he'd heard.

"Now see what I mean Margot. When you go digging up…" Einer began.

Margot said, "Oh, Ignatius, I don't want you to think that Matt didn't love Jill. Why he worshipped her. We all thought he'd go mad when she died. And he might have if his mother hadn't gone to Tennessee to help out. Jill and the boys were his life. What he felt for Caryn was youthful, undeveloped, intense. What he felt for Jill was mature, meaningful, profound. From the moment Matt met Jill, he loved her fiercely."

"Ironically, it was Caryn who introduced them," said Steve.

"I often thought that Caryn introduced them as a way to make up for choosing Hank over Matt," said Margot. "But regardless, from the time Matt laid eyes on Jill until she died, no one else mattered to him. So there's no reason to doubt Matt's love for Jill, Ignatius."

Ignatius nodded, satisfied.

Chapter 14

Audrey and Donald ate Chinese food and watched the traffic navigate through the flooded streets in Williamsburg Crossing Shopping Center. Procrastinators ventured out to snatch last minute food supplies, batteries, and jugs of water from near empty store shelves. A special electricity was present as the hurricane moved steadily toward town. An electricity born out of fear, excitement, and the emergence of some primitive survival instinct.

Traffic crept slowly over the rain-soaked streets. Fountains of water spewed upward through gutter grates and headlights created fascinating light patterns on the spray. On the restaurant windows steam from the kitchen framed a surreal scene outside. The restaurant was empty except for three Chinese employees and the two detectives.

Audrey and Donald had spent the afternoon going through city and county records that might provide a clue to the identification of Noah's birth parents. As was the case with adopted children, however, Will and Peedee were named as his parents. The date of his birth was the same date given by Doctor Harris and Ms. Simms, and place of birth was listed as simply James City County, Virginia.

"Waste of time?" Donald mumbled through mouthfuls of moo goo gai pan.

Audrey paused, a half-eaten egg roll suspended mid-air. "Now you sound like the Chief, Donald. No, it wasn't a waste of time. Suppose we hadn't examined those records and later on discovered that we'd missed some vital information. We'd feel like fools then. You never know what you'll find until you look." She stuffed the roll into her mouth and began to struggle into her rain slicker.

Donald followed suite. "You're right, of course. What I dread is this meeting with Einer Pellinger. Shouldn't we let him know we're coming?"

Audrey paused and cocked her head pensively. "No. Let's surprise him this time."

"He didn't like it when we showed up unannounced the other night."

"Well, this time is different," she smiled. "This time we're doing him a favor. We're giving him a chance to rebut a rumor."

"He intimidates the hell out of me."

"To be honest, he makes me anxious, too."

"*Really*?" Donald seemed reassured to know that he wasn't the only one frightened of Einer Pellinger. "You sure don't show it."

Audrey opened the door and braced herself against the wind. "Well I'm just a better actor than you, Donald."

"*Really?*"

* * *

Much to everyone's delight, Lexie had again created a culinary extravaganza. A cup of cucumber vichyssoise preceded a cherry salad served with an entrée of Southern fried chicken, spinach soufflé, and corn pudding. Hot home-baked rolls fairly floated from the breadbasket, and the meal was complete when fresh coconut cake was served with hot cappuccino. Following dinner, Lexie received her customary adulation from Einer, after which everyone filed into the library to view the latest report on Hurricane Jean.

The scenes that appeared on the television were of devastation, tragedy, and helplessness. Eastern North Carolina was crushed. How could aid reach the victims of this catastrophe in such ferocious wind and rapidly rising water? What lay ahead for James City County? Would it also be ravaged…homes demolished, businesses destroyed? The whole scenario was inconceivable, yet outside the wind was clearly gaining momentum and the rains were intensifying.

As the storm pummeled the house, the sound of the wind slowly changed. It no longer shrieked. Now it took on the resonance of a moan… like a frightened child groping at the doors and windows of the old mansion seeking refuge from the storm. Suddenly, the room was thrust into darkness and the television went silent. The abrupt sensory deprivation stunned the group. Then the silence was shattered as a melange of shrieks, gasps and screams exploded from the blackness.

"What the hell…" Ignatius's voice rose above the others.

"Take it easy everyone. Just a little interruption in the power," Einer said reassuringly.

A match was struck, and Ignatius' face appeared. The light gave temporary relief from the darkness, and everyone breathed a sigh of relief.

Einer continued. "If the power doesn't come on in a few seconds, the generator will kick in."

As if on command, power returned. The lights and television flickered a few times and then stayed on.

"I hope this is the most excitement we have tonight," said Carrie.

"Don't count on it," said Steve. Carrie shot him an angry look as if his doubts might cause more mishaps.

"Spirits exude electricity causing lights and electrical appliances to go on and off." It was Peedee speaking in a hushed voice. Her soft, round face possessed a serene look, and there was a distant, almost hypnotic look in her eyes. The group stared transfixed as she continued. "You know we are all made up of energy, and when we die that energy stays behind. That's what some people call..." she paused for effect, "the haunting phenomena."

"Steve..." Carrie's voice quivered and she grasped his arm.

"That does it," Steve said as he stood pulling Carrie up after him. "Time for us to go to bed. Let us know if anything disastrous is about to happen. Anything that's a natural disaster that is. Goodnight all." Carrie and Steve quickly left the room and disappeared up the stairs.

"Oh dear," said Peedee undeterred. "How unfortunate. People fear what they don't understand."

Peedee searched the room for a potential audience. Matt and Margot were already deeply engrossed in the television report, as if nothing had happened. Ben sat gaping at Peedee awaiting the next act. And Einer shook his head, walked to the bar, and poured himself another drink. "This is going to be one hell of a night," he said as he threw down a shot.

"Ignatius," said Einer. "Can I interest you..." He was interrupted by the sound of the door chimes resonating through the hall.

Ben jumped. "Scared the begeezus out of me."

"Who the hell's out this time of night and in this weather?" Einer swore.

As if in answer to his question, the maid entered the library. "Mr. Pellinger, it's those two detectives again."

"What?" he said as he charged toward the hall. "Never mind. I'll take care of this."

Audrey and Donald stood dripping onto the Oriental rug. They felt soaked and vulnerable. But when Audrey saw Einer's face flushed with anger, she suddenly experienced a rush of determination. Tonight they would not be answering to him as they had been when he stormed into the station. Tonight, they would be asking the questions, and Einer must answer them. And they had a copy of the note to produce the leverage.

"Aside from the stupidity of going out at night in the middle of a hurricane, what the hell are you doing at my home without calling first?" Einer demanded.

"I realize that calling first would have been more considerate," said Audrey. "But we have been so busy searching records that we forgot to follow the procedure you requested."

"Requested? I never *requested* a procedure. I damn well told you not to barge into my home unannounced again."

"Mr. Pellinger, sir," began Donald. He swallowed hard. "We have come into possession of some evidence that will most certainly be of interest, if not of concern, to you."

"What kind of evidence?"

"Perhaps it might be best to speak with us privately," said Audrey. Einer did not move. Rage consumed his face.

Then Margot appeared at the library door. "Einer, is something wrong? Audrey, Donald what a surprise to see you out on a night like this."

Einer's face was immediately transformed from anger to composure. "It's nothing, Margot." He spoke nonchalantly. "The detectives want to discuss some more details with me."

"Details?"

"Yes, dear," he said guiding her back towards the library. "I won't be long. Please attend to our guests. Perhaps some refreshments."

Margot returned to the library. Einer turned and faced squarely the two drenched detectives. "This better be good. Damned good," he said as he marched into the parlor.

Einer closed the large mahogany doors behind him. He then strode commandingly across the room and chose a mammoth, generously stuffed easy chair. He propped his feet upon its matching ottoman and motioned for the detectives to take a seat in two matching but less comfortable side chairs.

"How does Einer Pellinger always assume the commanding position?" thought Audrey.

Suddenly a distant crash, like a tree falling to the ground, shook the very foundations of Berryhill Plantation Mansion. The collapse was followed by a series of loud reverberations from somewhere within the house. The detectives started. Einer did not flinch.

Appearing totally unaffected Einer simply said, "Okay, let's have it."

Remembering the Chief's admonition, Audrey began, "Mr. Pellinger, when my partner and I returned to the office

135

today, there was a piece of mail addressed to Detectives Kelly and Anderson. The letter came through the post—in other words it was not hand-delivered. The writing was suspicious. It appeared to be disguised, so we handled it carefully so as not to destroy any evidence." Audrey paused. So far, so good she thought. Einer did not move. His face remained impassive.

Audrey cleared her throat and continued. "I'll read the note to you now, sir." She removed a piece of paper from her jacket pocket. "This is not the actual note, you understand. This is just a copy. But it is a photo copy."

Einer still said nothing but moved his hand in a gesture for Audrey to hurry along. Audrey fumblingly unfolded the paper and began to read. Damn, her voice quivered,

DETECTIVES KELLY AND ANDERSON...YOU HAVE BEEN TRYING TO FIND OUT WHO WAS NOAH MURRAY'S REAL MOTHER. WHY DON'T YOU ASK HIS REAL FATHER, EINER PELLINGER.
SOMEONE WHO WANTS TO HELP

Audrey looked up. She tried to clear her voice. It didn't work. Einer appeared completely controlled. He neither moved nor changed his expression. He said nothing.

"So," said Audrey, "that's the note."

"Is that all?" asked Einer.

"Well, y… yes sir," sputtered Audrey.

Einer moved as if he were about to stand. Donald found his voice and said, "Mr. Pellinger, since this is a murder investigation, and it appears that someone wants to involve you in this crime, we thought it best to come over here and give you an opportunity to respond to this accusation." Donald was pleased with himself.

"These records you alluded to earlier. Am I to surmise that they concerned Noah?" Einer asked.

"Yes, sir," Donald said. He was gaining confidence with each response.

"And?"

"We were checking to see if Noah's birth records gave any clue to his real birth parents."

Einer raised his shoulders and eyebrows to gesture, "And?"

"Nothing," Donald said. Almost immediately Donald realized that he had given Einer too much information, and Einer had given him none.

"Well, then I cannot see how this has anything to do with me." Einer stood and walked from the room. He tromped into the hall and straight to the front door. The detectives scurried behind him struggling to get into their slickers. He waited patiently as they nervously snapped their coats and lifted their hoods. He opened the door and with a feigned note of concern said, "Drive carefully." And he slammed the door sharply.

"Damn Donald. Why did you tell him that we found nothing in the records? He's a suspect for God's sake."

"Don't start on me, Audrey. How come you suddenly went mute back there?"

"Why? You want to know why? I'll tell you why, Donald," Audrey shouted above the wind and pelting rain. Then she lowered her voice to a mere whisper. Donald leaned forward to catch her words. She said, "I'm not as good an actor as I thought."

Chapter 15

"How strange," said Margot as she returned to the library. The others looked up questioningly. "That's Audrey and Donald, the police detectives. They came to discuss the investigation with Einer again. I can't imagine what's so urgent as to bring them out in this storm. One would think that policemen would be needed elsewhere tonight."

"Any idea what they want?" asked Matt.

"No, they didn't say…" her voice fading.

Peedee stood and moved slowly toward fireplace. She assumed an imposing posture and clasped her hands lightly in front of her. Her face took on a peaceful expression, and she spoke so softly that everyone was forced to become completely still in order to hear what she was saying.

"The spirits are active tonight," she began. "They acquire energy from the storm, and I feel that manifestations are likely to occur."

"Aunt Peedee, this is not the best time to entertain us with ghost stories," Matt admonished.

The ominous wind wailed like some phantom force assaulting the distant reaches of the house, and the walls moaned under the pressure of the storm. Somewhere outside a shudder became unhinged, freeing it to bang against the side of the building like a violent intruder. How many storms had this old house withstood in two hundred years? How many generations of Pellingers found shelter here? Had all that sought refuge within these walls survived the fury of the storms? Was their terror still entrapped in the walls and floors of the old mansion only to surface and merge with the fear of those experiencing tonight's dilemma? Suddenly a crashing sound jarred the house as somewhere in the woods another tree plummeted to the ground.

Gasps mingled with shrieks as the group reacted to the tremendous vibration.

"I thought that one had us," said Matt.

"Well, I can tell you one thing, Matt," said Ignatius, "I don't think much of your damned hurricane. This is my first, and I hope it's my last."

"*My* hurricane? Don't credit me with this storm," Matt said defensively.

Peedee cleared her throat, and all eyes again turned in her direction. She had not moved from the spot in front of the fireplace, and she remained calm. "Fear can have a gruesome effect on human behavior," she said quietly.

Peedee had their complete attention again. "I had a premonition that something extraordinary will take place tonight. All of the energy from the storm combined with the energy from past lives in this house set the stage for paranormal happenings."

Margot and Matt looked at Peedee dubiously. Ignatius shot her a glaring look of disdain, and Ben sat wide-eyed absorbing her every word.

"Oh, yes," Peedee continued, "We shall learn tonight just why my dear, kind son, Noah, died such a horrible death."

"No," Margot and Matt blurted out in unison.

Margot stepped forward and took her aunt's hand. "Aunt Peedee, please don't do this to yourself. Noah is gone, dear. And he would want you to let go and try to find peace."

Peedee gently patted Margot's hand. "Oh, Margot, you are afraid. It's okay to be afraid, dear. People fear what they don't understand. The point of death is very nebulous…legally, medically, and, of course, spiritually. Sometimes spirits just float around lost in time and space. And if they return to their loved ones, they have a reason."

Ben said, "Miz Peedee, what do you suppose Noah's reason would be to return here tonight?"

"Don't encourage this, Ben," whispered Ignatius. Ben appeared not to hear him and waited anxiously for Peedee's answer.

"I believe that Noah will return to identify his killer and reveal to us why he was murdered so viciously," she answered exactly.

Matt said, "Aunt Peedee, we *all* want Noah's killer found and punished but…"

Peedee interrupted, "I know, Matt. I know that we *all* want Noah's killer to be found, and that's why I think he will communicate with all of us."

"But," Matt continued, "that's why the police are here tonight. Aunt Peedee, *they* will find Noah's murderer."

"No, Matt, you're wrong. *We* will find his killer. And we'll find the killer in this very house. With Noah's help and the help of all the spirits of those who have lived here, we'll find his killer."

"Matt, make her stop," Margot whispered. Matt opened his mouth to speak.

Ben interrupted. "Now I think we're all getting upset over nothing. Miz Peedee don't have no problem with her gift. It's you who have a problem. People who have this gift were born with it. I know 'cause my mama had the gift of foreknowing. Didn't ever hurt her. Didn't ever hurt nobody. You folks just don't have confidence in Miz Peedee."

Ignatius shot Ben a look to kill. Then he looked at Matt. Matt simply shrugged.

"Thank you, Benjamin," Peedee said sweetly. "I'm not offended. Perhaps I can explain. Although I wasn't present at his birth, I've always felt that Noah was born with a veil over his face. People born with a veil over their face are blessed with the unusual ability to sense things that the rest of us can't. Even as a child, he could see and feel what others could not. He could look into your very soul. Knowing that Noah was blessed with this gift helped me to accept his other limitations. I accepted early on that his limitations were part of his karma, and after this life he would enjoy happier circumstances."

"Karma?" questioned Ignatius incredulously.

"Yes. Karma is moving from one life to another in an effort to achieve better circumstances in the next life. Noah's gift made this transitory life easier for him."

"Poppycock!" sputtered Ignatius.

"Now hold up, 'Natius," said Ben. "Now Miz Peedee, I don't know about this karma thing. Mama never talked about that."

"Oh, it's true, Benjamin. It's been proven through hypnosis. Many people have been regressed to their previous lives. It is felt that many of our fears, talents, and behaviors were carried over from a former life." Peedee

141

was delighted to have Ben as such an interested member of her audience.

Ben nodded as if he fully understood her explanation. Matt spoke skeptically, "Aunt Peedee, what does Noah's gift of precognition and this karma thing have to do with finding Noah's murderer."

"Matt, dear, because Noah possessed this supernatural proclivity, I know that his spirit is still here." She paused to allow them to absorb what she said. "And he knows how we are grieved by the brutal way he died. Noah will not go on to his next life until he helps us solve the mystery surrounding his death."

Ben's face took on a serious expression as he nodded. Margot struggled to hold back tears. Matt shook his head in disbelief, and Ignatius simply reached for his pipe. Soon he hid behind a thick cloud of tobacco smoke.

"There's really nothing to fear. We should embrace a haunting, as these manifestations are sometimes called. We should embrace them as a lifetime event," Peedee continued.

"How?" asked Matt. He was beginning to feel very uncomfortable with Peedee's role as psychic detective.

"What do we do next?" asked Ben expectantly. He was completely caught up in Peedee's performance.

Peedee moved confidently to a chair in front of the fire. Shadows from the flames danced eerily on her pale face. She sat silently for a moment then she spoke softly, "We must speak to Noah, Ben. Be aware there are many life forms and life forces. This room seems to be especially active, so we shall work here. And we mustn't be afraid. Ghosts, as we call them, are nothing more than spirits in trouble. As they want to help us, so we must help them."

For the first time, Ben seemed to be apprehensive. "Uh Miz Peedee, *how* are we going to speak to him?" he asked.

"We shall have a little séance," she responded simply.

"A *little* séance?" cried Margot incredulously.

"Ha!" bellowed Ignatius.

Peedee ignored the outburst. "Yes dear, Noah knows us so nothing elaborate is required."

"I don't believe this," Ignatius sneered.

"Hush up 'Natius," admonished Ben.

"Aunt Peedee, I'm not sure this is a good thing for you to do," cautioned Matt. "You've just been through a horrible ordeal with the funeral and the police interview. Shouldn't you wait …"

"Matt, experiences from the past are firmly imprinted on the present, especially in receptive environments such as this house," Peedee said. "And the victims in these experiences are most likely to manifest themselves if the event was a particularly violent one. If we uncover the events leading to Noah's demise, perhaps this would lead us to his murderer. A seance could be particularly impressive tonight because we could have a multiple witness event."

"Or a multiple illusion event," Ignatius derided.

"Well, count me in," said Ben. Any trace of wariness had vanished.

Peedee looked pleadingly at Margot and Matt.

"Well, if it will pacify you," Margot committed.

"Matt?" Peedee asked hopefully.

"Aunt Peedee, I don't know.."

"Please."

Matt hesitated, then said, "Well, okay. But I feel stupid," He added in an effort to save face with Ignatius.

Peedee looked at Ignatius questioningly. "Don't look at me," he growled. "I'll not lend credence to all this mumbo-jumbo by participating in some séance...big or little."

Peedee stood and stepped away from the fire. She held out her hands. "We must let Noah know that we are aware of his presence and that we need his guidance. And we must assure him that we'll work to bring his murderer to justice," Peedee directed. "Come take my hands, and we'll form a circle."

Margot reluctantly stepped forward and took one of her aunt's hands. Matt clasped Margot's hand protectively. Ben clumsily got to his feet and took Matt's hand in one hand and turned to Ignatius.

"Not on your life, Buddy," Ignatius growled. With that, Ben gently clasped Peedee's soft hand.

"There," said Peedee. "Now we must not break the circle, regardless of what happens. Understood?" The group mumbled their assent.

As if from the script of a ghost tale, trees began to screech and moan as the wind whipped through their branches ripping leaves and crashing small limbs to the ground. Creaks and groans were heard from far off rooms and chambers of the house, and the muffled sound of a clock struck somewhere in a distant corridor. A door or shudder slammed, freed from the latch intended to secure it. Then suddenly the house was cast into darkness. Gasps and cries filled the room.

"Not again," said Matt. Ignatius lit a match. Then a tremendous gust of wind swooshed down the chimney causing the fire to flare up. The light from the match mingled with the light from the fireplace creating a ghostly illumination.

"The generator will click on in a few minutes," Ignatius reminded them reassuringly.

The circle of four remained intact before the fireplace. "Let us proceed'" said Peedee. Peedee's face took on a peaceful expression. Her voice was soft and soothing. "Noah. Noah. This is your mother. We are here to help you, Noah."

The wail of the wind filled the house with sounds like sobs and groans, and the unrelenting rain pounded the roof. Matt tried to wrest his hands from Margot and Ben but their grips were firm.

"Noah, we are your loved ones. What do you want us to do? Tell us, Noah. We beg you to tell us what to do," Peedee implored.

Suddenly the library door burst open. The fire leapt high fed by the draft from the hallway. A huge figure filled the dark cavity of the doorway, and a powerful voice bellowed, "What the hell's going on in here?"

The members of the séance circle went limp. "Einer! How dare you frighten us like that!" Margot exclaimed, "Auntie Peedee is conducting a séance...like when Matt and I were kids."

"For Christ's sake, Margot," Einer said shaking his head and walking towards the bar. "Don't we have enough melodrama around here?"

"We most certainly do, Einer Pellinger, and so we don't need you to scare us to death by barging in here and shrieking like a banshee," Margot countered. She began to move about the room lighting candles.

Reaching for a fifth of bourbon, Einer poured himself a large drink. After a hefty swallow, he looked at Margot and shook his head. "My fault, dear. I should learn not to get alarmed when I find my wife participating in some kind of magic ritual."

"Magic ritual?" exclaimed Peedee. "Why Einer, how insulting. Do you really think I would become involved in magic? Magic is just superstition and tricks. There are scientific studies validating the credibility of seances."

Einer suddenly looked exhausted. "Peedee, I never meant to insult you. What did you hope to accomplish with a séance tonight?"

Peedee seemed mollified. "We were calling upon Noah to help us find his murderer. I know his spirit is here tonight. I just know it."

Einer sat down and lifted his feet onto an ottoman, he asked wearily, "How do you know that, Peedee?"

Peedee moved toward him her eyes begging him to believe her. "I dreamed it last night, Einer. I dreamed that Noah was here in this house and that he helped us find his murderer. I know we'll find his murderer." Einer took her hand and patted it gently.

Then Peedee lifted a flashlight and walked proudly toward the hallway. "Now if you will please excuse me, I must try to get some rest." She stopped at the doorway, turned and said, "We could have an extraordinary night ahead of us."

Matt turned to the others to explain, "When Margot and I were kids, we loved her stories, but we were also afraid of them. Guess nothing much has changed. She still frightens the..." he stopped abruptly and looked at Margot, "She still scares me."

Margot continued, "I remember how her imagination and stories engulfed us like a shroud." She faked a shiver. "It was fun to be scared back then. I'm not that brave any more."

"What weird behavior lurks in the gene pool of your family, Matt," Ignatius said derisively.

"Now let up on Miz Peedee. I ain't ready to throw her off yet," Ben said again defending Peedee.

Einer said exhaustedly, "Peedee may not be the brightest bulb in the marquee, but she's kind and generous, and she's a good judge of people."

Margot gave Einer's hand a hug. "You're just saying that because she idolizes you, Einer Pellinger."

They heard Peedee speak to someone at the top of the stairs and turned to see Steve and Carrie descending the steps flashlight in hand.

"Hey, Einer," Steve said as they entered the library. "What happened to the generator?"

"It appears to have malfunctioned, Steve. We've plenty of candles and battery-operated lamps."

At that moment, a maid entered the library carrying several flashlights, torches, and a box of candles. "Since the generator didn't come on, sir, I thought you'd need these."

"Thank you, and tell the staff that they may all turn in now. We'll keep an eye on things tonight," Einer said.

Matt distributed the flashlights.

"What's been going on down here?" asked Steve sleepily.

Glancing at Carrie, Matt replied quickly, "Not much, Einer had a visit from the police."

Steve was immediately alert. "What? At this time of night?" he questioned.

"Just an update on their investigation," added Einer cautiously. "Margot dear, why don't you and Carrie go on up to bed. I'll be up shortly. I need to make sure that everything is secure."

Margot suddenly looked exhausted. "Carrie, that sounds like a good idea to me."

"I don't know," Carrie hesitated. "No offense, Einer...I really appreciate your hospitality, but your house gives me the creeps."

Einer laughed. "No offense taken. I've lived here so long that I tend to forget that it can be daunting to some people. Tell you what... Margot, why don't you keep Carrie company until Steve comes up? I don't think any of us will get much sleep tonight anyway."

"Good idea. Come on Carrie," Margot said steering Carrie towards the hallway. "If this house has withstood two hundred years of hurricanes, I'm sure we'll make it through tonight."

"It's not the hurricane that scares me," Carrie said yielding reluctantly to Margot's lead, "it's what's inside."

Chapter 16

Margot and Carrie disappeared up the stairs, and the men sat silently for a long time. Einer's guests were reluctant to intrude on their host's thoughts although they were teeming with curiosity to know why the police detectives' had come out tonight. The glow from the fireplace combined with the flicker of candlelight created a solemn, almost hypnotic, aura in the room. It seemed inappropriate to speak for fear of spoiling the subdued mood.

Outside the safe haven of the library, a steady, relentless wind continued to batter the trees. Limbs writhed as if attempting to shield themselves from the destruction being visited upon them. The pounding of the rain in tandem with the heightening wind created conditions that were becoming increasingly perilous. Yet the five men sat silently, expectantly, while Einer stared into the fluttering flames. Finally Einer stirred, and the others straightened, alert and hopeful.

"Only a dammed fool would come out on a night like this," Einer declared. He received murmurs of assent.

Ignatius and Ben waited patiently for they did not feel it was their place to encourage Einer to confide in them. Another period of silence followed. Then finally Matt said, "Einer, what was so important that the police came here tonight?"

Einer looked at his empty glass. "You know, I think I've been drinking too much. Need to cut back some," he said as he moved unsteadily towards the bar. "I'll give that some thought tomorrow."

"You mean they came all the way out here to tell you that you're drinking too much?" Steve teased.

Einer smiled and poured himself a drink. "No Steve, they didn't come out here to tell me that I'm drinking too much. They came to tell me that they think I murdered Noah."

"What?" gasped Matt and Steve in unison. Ignatius snorted, and Ben inched to the edge of his seat.

Ben looked Einer straight in the eye, and said, "Einer, now you tell us 'xactly what they said."

Einer began, "It seems that the detectives received an anonymous letter through the mail claiming that I was Noah's natural father." The faces of his friends registered shock. Einer returned to his chair and continued, "It also seems that the two detectives spent most of the day attempting to find some evidence to verify or refute this claim. Apparently having found no such verification or refutation, they made the decision to confront me directly under the guise of giving me a chance to comment on the note."

"And did you? Comment that is?" asked Ben.

"No," said Einer.

"Of course not," Steve exclaimed heatedly. "Einer, Noah's father? Why that accusation doesn't even pass the giggle test. If this is how those stupid cops are going to run this investigation, they'll never find Noah's killer."

"Now ease up, Steve," cautioned Ben. "Those two police detectives were just doing their job. They have to check out every piece of evidence no matter how incredible it might be."

"Are you taking their part in this just because you're a sheriff?" Steve asked angrily.

"Steve," Einer interrupted forcefully. "That will be quite enough…"

"That's okay, Einer," Ben said. "Steve, I ain't got no dog in this fight. I'm just saying that where murder is concerned, a policeman has to investigate everything, and you can't fault them personally."

Steve looked embarrassed. "Sorry, Ben. I didn't mean to question your intentions. I'm just so damned drained. What with the death of Noah, the funeral, Peedee, and now Carrie's about to lose it because she thinks the house is haunted… I'm really sorry," he repeated.

Ben placed his hand on Steve's shoulder. "That's okay, Steve, I understand that things have been…."

"We've digressed again!" exploded Ignatius. "Can't we ever stick to the subject at hand which in this case happens to be the police's visit with Einer?"

Ben returned to his sheriff's mode. "I agree. I've always believed that the fires of evil are sparked by rumors. Einer tell us exactly what was said."

"Of course," replied Einer, and he repeated verbatim the entire interview.

Einer's monologue was followed by silence. Interestingly enough, everyone looked to Ben for the next move. Finally Sheriff Day said in an official manner, "Then am I right in assuming that you neither confirmed nor denied the paternity claim made in the letter?"

"That's right," answered Einer.

"Why, Einer?" asked Matt. "Why not just deny it, and then they won't waste their time on some bogus lead."

"I couldn't deny it, Matt," he said. "I couldn't deny it because it's probably true."

The men stirred uncomfortably. Only Ben remained unflappable. He suggested cautiously, "Want to tell us about it?"

Einer stared into the fire. He spoke as if he were talking to himself. "When I was a young man, my father had great ambition for me. Having no siblings made it particularly difficult to singularly live up to all his expectations. An ivy-league education was only a part of my training. I was also instructed in politics, not from the standpoint of becoming an elected official myself, but from the standpoint of being the person behind the elected official. I was taught that therein, lies power. I also learned every intricate aspect of my father's business. I could work every job from pushing a broom to dealing with employee disputes, and I spent my summers honing these skills. No, sir. No foolish trips abroad or frivolous parties for Einer Pellinger. In the summer, my classroom moved from the university to my father's business."

Einer had a far-away look in his eye. No one moved. Steve and Matt had never heard Einer speak so personally, and they found it fascinating that a powerful man like Einer experienced such adversities too.

Einer continued, "One summer my father assigned me a problem concerning one of his workers. The worker was a janitor. It seemed that the man was not very bright, and other employees were making his life miserable by teasing him. So the old fellow decided to quit his job. My assignment was to get the other workers off the old man's back, and talk him into staying on the job. Now, my father was a demanding man, and he *would* have things his way, but I'll say this much for him…One, he treated all his workers with respect. And two, if anyone left their job it would be his decision, not theirs nor anyone else's."

"Sounds like your father ran a tight ship," remarked Ignatius.

"That he did, Ignatius. It wasn't difficult to stop the teasing. A mere threat of losing their job brought the bullies back into line, because being fired by my father meant that a worker would be black balled from other jobs around here. However, talking the old man into staying would be hard. He'd been humiliated. So I drove out to his place to placate him. When I got there, he was loading his few belongings into a beat up old truck. I introduced myself and made every argument I could think of to persuade him not to quit. Finally, he agreed to stay. I reached out my hand to shake his and looked over his shoulder to the porch." Einer paused and then continued breathlessly, "There stood one of the most beautiful girls I'd ever seen in my life. She didn't look real. She didn't wear make-up and her blonde hair was pulled back into a long ponytail, and she had the most beautiful smile. She looked like a porcelain doll. Unfortunately, Mary, like her father, was terribly simple. You see she lived alone with him, and she'd had little contact with other people. I decided that anyone that frail and helpless needed someone to care for her, to protect her. I decided to be that someone."

Einer paused again, a distant look in his eyes. "I asked the old man's permission to take her on picnics, for rides, and such. He consented although I could tell that he was reluctant. But after all, how do you say no the boss's son. So I began a summer romance. As nature would have it, my desire to protect her evolved into a sexual desire. Young love can be intense, and our appetites were insatiable. Early on, I even entertained fantasies of marrying Mary. She would be my Pygmalion."

Einer paused and scrutinized his empty glass. No one spoke. He placed the glass on the table and sighed. "But as with most summer romances, it ended. Mary cried, and I returned to the university. I thought of her so many times that winter. I'll not have you think that I never had feelings for her," he added sternly. "But the distance between us allowed me an opportunity to view the affair more realistically. I decided that it would be kinder not to see her again. When the next summer rolled around, I threw myself into the agenda my father planned for me. I still thought of Mary especially when it was so damned hot that only a midnight swim in the river brought relief. My feelings were not simply the result of a youthful flow of testosterone. I still had deep affection for Mary, and I thought obsessively of the previous summer. I suppose this is not unusual for a first love affair."

Einer interrupted his story and cleared his throat. This was not easy for him. Years of silence made it painful to reveal a secret that he'd hidden for so long. He rubbed his eyes and squinted to refocus. Still no one spoke. Finally Einer continued. "One night my father gave a dinner party. The conversation turned to a pathetic young girl who died giving birth to a baby boy. The baby was born at home with only the girl's father in attendance. Stunned, I realized with horror that the girl they were talking about was Mary. The old man was taking care of the child. He still worked for my father as a janitor, and he brought the baby to work with him every day in a basket. Strangely, it seemed that the baby never cried. Much to my horror some of our dinner guests felt that social services should be alerted and the baby taken from his grandfather. I felt panic. I couldn't bear the thought of the old man losing Mary and the baby. Later when our guests left, I suggested to my father that he allow me to handle the problem of the old man and the child. I reminded him that I'd worked with the old man the previous summer. My father never made a decision quickly, and he thought about this for what seemed to be an eternity. Finally one day, he called me in and simply said, 'take care of it'. Just like that…'take care of it'. I knew that baby was probably my son."

Einer paused again. The men sat silently in deference to his tragic story, while outside the wind wailed as if in requiem to Mary's short, hopeless life.

"So you were responsible for Noah being placed with his foster parents," Ben stated.

"Yes. I didn't want to lose him in the labyrinth of foster care," continued Einer. "I knew the Birdsongs to be kind and caring people. They had been foster parents for many children. Although they were getting old, they were willing to take handicapped children that other foster parents refused. Noah was the last foster child they ever took in…they're both dead now. Any way, I followed through to make sure there would be no records to trace Noah to Mary, her father, and of course me. There was no problem with Social Services, and the Birdsongs agreed to take Noah.

"Then I went to see Mary's father. I'll never forget the look on the old man's face when I drove up. He was terrified. I asked to see the baby, and he just nodded. He walked inside and came out with a basket and held it up for me to see. The baby was inside. He was so strange looking. He was emaciated and neither moved nor cried. Tears came into the old man's eyes and his voice quivered. He just said, 'He's a good baby. He don't cry'. I realized then that he was afraid that I was going to tell him that he couldn't bring the baby to work. I quickly explained that I hadn't known that Mary had a baby, and that I just learned of her death. I reassured him that I came to help him. And do you know what happened? He collapsed. Yes, he collapsed with relief. He sat on the steps and cried like a baby. I tried to console him. I told him about the Birdsongs and their willingness to take Noah. And I assured him that he could see the baby anytime he wanted. He wept the whole time I was talking, and when I asked him if the arrangement would be agreeable to him, he grabbed my hand and kissed it. That's right…he actually kissed my hand."

"I know that made you feel good…him being appreciative and all," said Ben.

"No Ben, it made me feel like a son of a bitch," Einer responded.

"Then you don't know for sure if Noah was your child?" asked Ignatius again steering the conversation away from feelings to fact.

"Am I positive? No, Ignatius I can't say I'm positive. There wasn't the certainty of DNA at that time. And I was too fearful of what the less definitive tests would show. Hell, I was still a kid myself. Later on I rationalized that I was doing all I could for Noah so why bring it up at all."

Steve said, "Well, I can understand that, Einer. Sometimes it's best to let sleeping dogs lie."

"Problem with that philosophy is that sometimes those sleeping dogs wake up and take a bite out of your ass," Ignatius asserted.

"Have you ever told anyone this story?" asked Ben.

"Not a soul," replied Einer.

"Did the Birdsong's know that Noah might be your son?" asked Ben.

Einer stirred uncomfortably. "I never told them, but they knew that I was responsible for his foster placement. I mean I cut through a lot of red tape they'd had to go through when they took in other foster children. They also agreed to let Mary's father visit, and he visited right up until he died."

"In other words, you think they may have guessed?" asked Ignatius.

"Perhaps," said Einer uncertainly.

"Or her father may have told them about your affair with Mary," said Matt.

"I'll bet that's it," exclaimed Steve. "I'll bet Mr. and Mrs. Birdsong with the help of Mary's father put two and two together and figured out that Einer is his father."

"*Could* be his father," corrected Ignatius.

"Well, that's just well and good," mused Ben, "but there's one thing wrong with the conclusion that the Birdsongs or Mary's father tipped the police."

"What's that?" asked Matt who had been unusually quiet during the story.

"What's wrong is that they're all dead," Ben said. "We need to be looking to the living to find the one who wrote that note."

"That's right. But what if Einer is Noah's biological father? If he wanted to get rid of Noah, why wait all these years? It doesn't make sense," said Matt.

"Yeah, and who wrote the damn note? And why?" asked Steve.

Einer was a private man. He was accustomed to giving help and advice, not asking for it. Ben was far less educated and worldly than Einer. It wasn't pride that made it difficult for Einer to ask Ben's help, it was lack of experience. But Einer had a keen eye for resourcefulness and intuitiveness, and Ben caught that eye. Einer valued Ben's opinion.

"So Ben," Einer said hesitatingly. "What do you think I should do?" Einer always spoke decisively, so everyone was surprised to detect uncertainty in his voice.

"Einer, I ain't one to give you advice, but whatever you decide to do, don't do it lessen you have a lawyer there," Ben cautioned. Einer nodded.

The hurricane appeared to be approaching full force. Branches knocked savagely against the house as if trying to get in. And the wind threatened to violate the sanctuary where many generations of Pellingers had sought shelter from storms blown in from the raging sea. The wind no longer shrieked. It moaned like a lost soul being tortured in some distant corridor or secret room of the ancient house. Just outside the library, a figure lurked in an unlit corner of the hallway. The dark form had clasped a hand over its mouth and listened silently as Einer recounted his youthful saga. When Einer finished, the shadow slowly emerged, and Peedee crept quietly towards the stairs.

Chapter 17

Peedee crept cautiously past Carrie's room. She could hear Margot's muffled voice. "This house is not haunted, Carrie. It's just drenched in history and family legends."

Peedee was not ready to share the story she'd just heard downstairs. She needed time to sort through her ambivalent feelings. Noah's death had left her feeling drained and powerless. Since Will's death, she'd relied on Einer to take care of her business and personal problems. And when Noah was murdered, she was confident that Einer would pursue the murderer until he was apprehended and punished. But now, she'd learned that Einer could be Noah's real father. Would this make Einer reluctant to allow the police to dig too deeply? How would knowing that Einer was Noah's father impact her relationship with Einer?

Peedee stole silently into her room. She breathed a sigh of relief and closed the door quietly behind her. Groping about in the darkness she reached a table and found a candle there. Then fumbling in her pocket she took out a match. The strike was followed by a welcomed flicker of light that intensified when the candlewick was ignited. Peedee carried the candle to the window and set it upon a table. Fluffing the pillows on the small loveseat she sat down and drew an afghan tightly about her shoulders. Suddenly Peedee felt completely flattened.

The wind rattled the windows threatening to crash into her snug chamber. But most remarkable were the sheets of rain that streamed down the glass almost obscuring the yard and woods below. Peedee had intended to ask Steve or Matt to secure her shutters tonight. Now knowing what Einer had confided in them would make conversation with them very awkward. She must come to terms with what she'd overheard. After all, Einer's affair with Mary happened so long ago. Einer was very young…probably eighteen, nineteen. Mary, for all practical purposes, was a child herself. Noah an innocent baby. She began to reason. Had Einer's parentage diminished his efforts to help Noah over the years? No. Did Peedee's knowledge of this relationship change the kind, unselfish person Einer is? No. Peedee sighed out loud. "I'm simply too tired to think." She lay her head against the back of the loveseat and closed her eyes. She listened as the wind moaned and battered the house.

"Noah, Noah," she whispered. "What would you have me do dear? I need your kind and loving counsel tonight. Please tell me what to do."

She sat up slowly and gazed intently into the dark yard and woods below. She watched the trees lash each other and strip tattered leaves from the branches and send them swirling into the wind. All the trees waved savagely except one. It stood perfectly still. Then slowly, very slowly, it moved away from the others. And bent against the wind, an ethereal form crept stealthily toward the house.

Peedee leaned forward and pressed the palm of her hand against the windowpane and whispered, "Noah. Oh, Noah, I knew you'd come. I knew it."

Peedee reached down and found her purse that lay on the floor next to the loveseat. After rummaging inside, she extracted her cell phone and dialed the James City County Police Department.

* * *

Audrey and Donald found the drive back to James City County police station fraught with obstacles. Boughs of uprooted trees stretched across John Tyler Highway forcing their car to drive onto a shoulder that was now comparable to quick sand. Limbs and leaves covered the road, and the highway was a veritable minefield of hazardous debris. In spots, the road was completely flooded. The police car hydroplaned once, and its motor stalled twice. Audrey and Donald alternated between swearing and praying although neither could be heard above the roar of the wind and the pounding of the windshield wipers.

The drive took about three times longer than it usually did. When the detectives finally turned into the parking lot of the police station, they almost collapsed with relief. Only three cars were in the lot. The others would be answering calls. Audrey and Donald made a dash for the station and hopefully a cup of hot coffee. The policeman behind the front desk lifted his head with a glazed and harried look on his face. They recognized him as the same officer who had been working that morning.

"Bob not here yet?" asked Donald.

"Here and gone," was the weary reply. "Everybody's out of pocket tonight. I'm pulling another shift."

Donald and Audrey were pouring large cups of thick, dark coffee. "It's coming down in buckets out there. I swear I think the rain is more of a problem than the wind," said Audrey.

"I know," said the officer behind the desk. "They got a real mess over on Jamestown Road. A dam broke and a bunch of cars and houses are flooded out. They're moving some residents to the shelter at William and Mary College."

"Damn," swore Donald. "That's too bad. Where's the Chief?"

"Your guess is as good as mine. Want me to try to raise him?"

"Give us a minute," said Audrey. "Any calls for us?"

"Well, as a matter of fact there was one," the officer replied as he shuffled through notes on his desk. "Weren't you just out at Berryhill? What the hell I do with that...oh, here it is. Someone called—the connection was not too good. Cell phone I think. Said her name was Peewee..."

"Peedee," Audrey corrected excitedly.

"Well, whatever," the desk officer continued caustically. "Anyway she said something like Noah's killer was going to be there tonight. Something about not breaking a circle and getting help from the departed. Hell, I couldn't make any sense of it. She might have been drunk for all I know. I've had so many calls tonight..."

The exhausted officer didn't have a chance to finish his complaints. Audrey and Donald pulled on their slickers and darted back out into Hurricane Jean.

They knew the drive back to Berryhill would be more hazardous than the trip they just made, but they never

162

realized how much more hazardous. Only minutes had passed since they navigated this road. Incredibly even more water covered the highway.

"I don't know if we can make it, Audrey," muttered Donald.

"We've got to try," Audrey argued determinedly.

"Hell, we don't even know what Peedee's talking about. She's an old lady full of grief. She might be hallucinating. Why don't we just call out there and check on her? They've obviously got a cell phone."

"And tip them off that we're coming? Not on your life, Donald. Damn!" The car skidded. Audrey regained control.

"That was close! Good going, Audrey!" Donald shouted above the pounding of the rain against the squad car.

Outside the specious safety of the car, the wind moaned, and trees branches swayed violently. Suddenly there was an explosion. Somewhere in the woods a tree collapsed, its roots no longer able to anchor it in the muddy soil. The vibration shook the car violently. The rain created a greater danger than the wind. The overflow from ditches and creeks concealed the road, and Audrey was left with the sensation of navigating a boat. The car hydroplaned relentlessly often resulting in complete lack of control over the vehicle. The wipers groaned torturously in an effort to beat off shredded leaves and thunderous raindrops that pounded the windshield in torrents. When the car stalled the wipers stopped working, and instantly an impenetrable black curtain of rain blanketed the windshield making it impossible to see anything. Audrey managed to start the car again, but success was short lived. After traveling only a few yards, a gigantic dark barricade suddenly loomed across the road. Audrey slammed on the brakes causing the car to go into a skid at a forty five-degree angle. The vehicle fishtailed and banged broad side into a tremendous pine tree that lay sprawled across the road. Donald and Audrey were jolted brutally. The airbags inflated instantly smacking the detectives smartly.

"Dam!" swore Audrey. "Donald you okay?"

Donald groaned. "Yeah. I always wondered what it'd feel like to have one of these things go off."

"Now you know. What do we do next?" she wondered aloud.

Donald was already extricating himself from the bag and safety belt. "Can't think of any choice that appeals to me."

"Me either," Audrey said as she freed herself. "We could call back to the station, but the Chief wouldn't be happy about dispatching someone to help us when things are as busy as they are tonight. Especially since neither one of us is hurt."

"You're right. I'd feel like a damned fool having to be rescued myself. We'll just have to hoof it," Donald reasoned.

"I agree," said Audrey. A wry smile suddenly crept onto her face. "However, it seems to me we've passed the point of no return."

"What do you mean?" asked Donald, recognizing that look.

"I mean that it's farther back to the station than it is to Berryhill."

"You mean walk to Berryhill? We don't know what's going on, Audrey, and Lord only knows what condition we'll be in when we get there. There could be a problem, but we also know that Peedee is a nut case. I'm not sure about this."

"I still say Berryhill," said Audrey. "If for no other reason, we stand a better chance of making it there than getting back to the station."

"I suppose you're right," Donald agreed reluctantly. He began to think out loud. "We'll need to stay on the road not the shoulder, and watch for downed power lines and other dangerous debris. In low areas around creeks, water gets pretty rough and high. If it looks too deep or swift, we'll just come back to the car and stay put. We don't want to try to be heroes."

Audrey gave Donald a tired look and said sarcastically, "No, Donald. We don't want to try to be heroes." She was fastening her slicker and pulling up the hood. "Now the coach road is about a mile or so up the road. Surely we can make that. Once we get onto the coach road, the trees and undergrowth in the woods should act as somewhat of a windbreak and give us a little protection. As for the rain, we'll just have to deal with it."

And deal with it they did. With great difficulty they pushed open the doors of the car and stepped into water that reached above their ankles. They were lashed with wind gusts so strong that it banged the car doors shut and threatened to rip off their rainwear. Slowly they trod in the direction of Berryhill. But it was the rain that was the greatest deterrent. Enormous drops peppered their faces. The sting was so great that they squinted to protect their eyes. Strands of Audrey's hair escaped from her hood and lashed her face furiously. The arduous trek seemed to take forever. They finally reached the coach road, and after fording mud holes that had grown to the size of small ponds, they determined where the main path must be. As Audrey had surmised, the small trees and undergrowth in the woods on each side the coach road provided a windshield. They even experienced some relief from the rain as the enormous oak trees canopied the coach road liked gigantic umbrellas. Although it was still less than easygoing, they gained some protection from the elements. Slowly they plodded through the tunnel of trees in the direction of the house.

* * *

The men sat quietly before the blazing fire. The flickering glow illuminated the room and created eerie shadows that danced from the corners and leapt from behind furniture. Conversation ceased. Steve dozed with his chin in his hand. Ben nodded and then jerked awake. Matt and Einer stared into the fire intently as though a solution to this problem might appear in the flames.

Ignatius spoke. "What the hell are we waiting for?" The others stared at him questioningly. "I mean is this what you do during a hurricane? Just sit around and wait? What are we waiting for?"

The men laughed releasing the tension that had built up following Einer's story.

Matt said, "We're not waiting for anything, Ignatius. Just seems rather pointless to go to bed. Every time you hear a crash you have to get up and check it out. If the wind or rain gets in the house, it can cause a lot of damage. Might as well just stay up. I can remember when we were young we used to stay up all night. We had hurricane parties. Remember that, Steve?"

"Sure do," Steve said sleepily. "A bunch of us would get together and get a few kegs of beer and some fast women..."

"What ?" coughed Matt.

"Oh, did I say fast women? I meant fast music. And we'd dance all night. We could out rock any hurricane...even Hazel. Remember Hurricane Hazel Einer?"

"I'm not likely to forget her. She was a rough one, Steve. Now wind was more of the culprit than rain during Hazel." Suddenly thunderous pounding came from the hallway and interrupted Einer. "Why someone's banging on the front door. Who the hell is out tonight?" He started to stand up.

Ben stopped him, "No, Einer. You let me get this one. Ain't no telling what kind of crazy's out on a night like this."

Ben reached for a flashlight and followed its beam down the hall. He placed his ear against the door. "Who is it?" he shouted.

"The police." The response was less confident than the detectives would have liked.

Ben threw open the door. Standing before him rain soaked and wind beaten were Audrey and Donald. A wide grin slowly stretched across Ben's face. Looking Audrey straight in the eye he said, "Well, lookeee here!"

Chapter 18

Audrey and Donald stood in puddles of water before the fire. Five pairs of eyes stared at them incredulously. They removed the rain gear that had done little to protect them. Wet, matted hair hung in their faces, and their uniforms were soaked and stuck to their skin. Audrey looked down and saw that her clinging wet shirt revealed her voluptuous qualities. "I feel like I'm in a wet tee shirt contest," she thought. Neither detective spoke. Their teeth chattered so hard that they feared they'd crack, and they shivered convulsively.

"Get them some brandy," snarled Einer. Matt went to the bar and poured two generous portions of brandy. He handed a glass to each detective. Donald took a hefty swallow and sputtered vigorously.

Audrey refused the glass saying, "No thank you. I'm on duty."

"Bull shit," growled Ignatius. "Don't be a damned fool. You're shaking all over."

"He's right," said Ben genuine concern in his voice. "You want to come down with pneumonia?"

Audrey reached for the glass. Her hand was shaking so badly that brandy splashed onto the hearth.

"Here," said Steve, trying hard not to stare at Audrey's transparent shirt, "you better sit down." He pulled a chair close to the fire. Audrey collapsed into it.

"What the hell are you two doing out again tonight? What's so important that it can't wait until morning?"

Einer demanded. "I think your Chief needs to find a keeper for you two. Of all the stupid things…"

Ben interrupted Einer's tirade. "Donald suppose you tell us what brought you two out again tonight in the middle of this hurricane? You know you could have been killed."

Donald looked at Audrey. Usually she took the lead, but she was exhausted by their ordeal. "Well, Sheriff," he began. Audrey shot him a look of disdain. "When we got back to the station, we had a message that there was an emergency here."

"What? An emergency?" repeated Ben.

"What kind of emergency?" asked Steve.

"And who called?" added Matt.

Donald looked at his empty glass. No one offered to refill it. "The message really didn't make sense, but we had to check it out. It was from Mrs. Peedee."

"Huh," snorted Ignatius. "No wonder, it didn't make sense. Nothing that woman says makes sense."

"Now hold up 'Natius," said Ben. "Why don't you tell us just 'xactly what the message said."

"The officer on duty wasn't completely sure that he got it right. There was something about Noah's murderer coming here tonight. And the weird part was about getting help from the dead or something like that," Donald looked embarrassed realizing how foolish it sounded.

"Geez," said Steve as he covered his face and shook his head.

The commotion downstairs had not gone unnoticed. Carrie and Margot peeped down the stairwell in time to see Ben escort the two detectives into the library. They rushed to Peedee's room to tell her that the police were here again, and to their amazement, Peedee was not surprised.

Together the three women descended the stairs and entered the library just in time to hear Donald's explanation of why they had ventured out in the middle of the hurricane.

"Aunt Peedee," Margot scolded. "How could you do something so reckless?" The men had not noticed the women entering the library and turned abruptly at the sound of Margot's voice.

Einer walked quickly to Margot. He took her hands in his and said, "Now it's nothing to be upset about, dear. Nothing serious has happened. Peedee's just distraught. It's unfortunate that the police came out again tonight, but they are okay so there's no real harm done."

Audrey seemed to recover, and she stood up shakily. "Why don't we let Mrs. Murray tell us if anything serious has happened? Mrs. Murray, did you call the station tonight?"

Peedee struck a confident pose. "I most certainly did," she answered emphatically. Margot and Carrie gasped.

"Is there something important you would like to tell us?" Audrey asked.

"There certainly is," Peedee answered looking squarely at Einer. Einer turned pale, but his persona remained resolute.

Audrey caught the look that passed between them and continued quickly, "What do you want to tell us Mrs. Murray?" she asked expectantly.

"I want to tell you that I have spoken to Noah, and I asked him to help us identify his murderer tonight. I thought you should be here to make the arrest," Peedee replied simply.

"What?" Audrey was flabbergasted. She stumbled backward toward the fireplace. Donald reached out to steady her. He gawked at Peedee.

"Oh, no," groaned Matt.

"Oh, God," said Ignatius, "Peedee's dreamed up a ghost for herself."

"Aunt Peedee tell me you didn't have these police officers come all the way back out here in the middle of a hurricane to tell them that you've contacted Noah through some kind of séance," Steve blurted.

"Séance?" Audrey repeated. Now she was completely dumbfounded.

"I most certainly did," Peedee said irrefutably.

"You mean Donald and I came all the way to Berryhill in the middle of a hurricane on an emergency call precipitated by a séance? Do you know what we went through to get here? Do you even know that there is a hurricane out there?" Audrey's voice was loud and shrill. She stepped toward Peedee.

Ben caught her by the arm. "Whoa there little lady," he said. "Let's hear Miz Peedee out."

"Thank you, Ben," said Peedee. "You're always so considerate. Perhaps you will feel less resentful Detective Kelly if I assure you that your trip was not in vain."

"And *how* can you give me that assurance, Mrs. Murray?" Audrey asked vehemently.

"Because I know there will be an intervention tonight. I know that Noah is here to help us," Peedee explained.

Audrey swore. "Now hold on, hold on," cautioned Ben. "How do you know Noah's here?"

"You're encouraging her again," muttered Ignatius. "I tell you, she's on the lunatic fringe."

Peedee ignored Ignatius. "I know Noah is here, because I saw him." Dramatically, she paused for effect then added softly, "Tonight as I sat in my room, I called out to him to help us find his murderer. And then I looked down into the front yard, and there was Noah coming toward the house. Coming to help us." Her voice was becoming desperate. "Don't you see Detective Kelly, I had to let you know that tonight is the night. The night we'll find out who murdered Noah, and I desperately wanted *you* to be the one to make the arrest."

With a groan Audrey collapsed onto the chair by the fireplace. From across the room Carrie shrieked, "Steve, now! I want to leave now…if we have to go in a boat."

Pandemonium broke out. Steve moved quickly to console Carrie. Audrey, Donald, and Ben all talked at the same time. Matt and Margot berated themselves for participating in Peedee's séance, and Ignatius clouded the issue further by blowing voluminous clouds of rank-smelling smoke from his pipe. After a few moments of chaos, Einer intervened.

He used a commanding tone, yet lowered his voice. Everyone was forced to stop talking in order to hear what he was saying. "Carrie, I won't hear of you traveling out on a night like this. Only a very foolish person would do that." He looked squarely at Audrey and Donald. "Steve will be with you all night, and you'll be safe. Peedee, your family and friends understand your grief and your need to obtain closure to Noah's tragic death. I promise you, you will have that closure. But no more emergency phone calls. The police take them damn seriously. As for you

172

Detectives Kelly and Anderson, there is no other choice but that you should remain here until the storm abates. Margot will show you to a room."

Audrey said, "Thank you but..."

Donald interrupted Audrey. "Thank you Mr. Pellinger. We'd be grateful if you'd let us stay until morning. But don't fix a room for us. If it's okay with you, we'll just sit here in front of the fire. I could sleep standing up."

"Have it your way. Margot, shall we go on up? Steve, Carrie?"

The two couples walked to the hall. When they reached the door, Einer turned and said, "Peedee, don't you think you should get some rest?" He waited for her. She quickly crossed the room and took his arm reaffirming their bond.

"Well that goes for me, too," said Ignatius. His eyes scanned the room and they soon fell on a ball of white fur cowering in a corner. Pete was terrified of the wind and rain. The pitiful dog had spent the last few days hiding in closets and under furniture in an effort to escape the sounds of the storm.

"Come on, Pete," said Ignatius slapping his leg. "Let's go to bed." The dog sped across the room and jumped onto Ignatius lap. Trembling, he buried his head in the pit of Ignatius' arm. "Coming Ben?" he added as an afterthought.

"Later," replied Ben.

Ignatius glanced at Audrey. Then he rolled his eyes and steered his chair toward the dark hall. Following the beam of his flashlight, he headed in the direction of his room.

Matt spoke, "Detectives Kelly and Anderson, could I speak to you about my Aunt Peedee?"

"That's why we're here, Mr. Murray…to listen. And it seems like we got all night," replied Audrey.

Matt pulled a chair to face Audrey. He leaned forward and began, "You see, Peedee has always been intrigued with the paranormal. My Uncle Will found it appealing for some strange reason. My Grandmother and Grandfather were tolerant, and my cousins and I found it entertaining. We never stopped to analyze it. To us it was harmless fantasy. Even Noah found it non-threatening and entertaining. I suppose that over the years she became a little too obsessed. Do you understand what I mean?"

"Yes, I understand, Mr. Murray," said Audrey, "but why are you telling me this?"

"I just don't want you to think that Aunt Peedee was playing a prank in bringing you out here tonight. She hasn't got a calculating bone in her body."

"Oh, I don't think Mrs. Murray was pulling a prank on us tonight, Mr. Murray. I think your aunt had a legitimate reason for calling us out here tonight, and I intend to find out what that reason is," Audrey said emphatically.

Matt was taken aback. "Well," he sputtered, "I wish you luck. We all want to find Noah's killer."

"And we're going to do everything we can to help," Audrey quipped.

Matt turned and left the library. Ben stared at Audrey, a twisted smile on his face.

"What?" Audrey asked.

"Oh, I was just wondering why you took off on my buddy Matt like that. Most folks think he's a mighty fine fellow," Ben grinned.

"I'm not judging a congeniality contest here, Sheriff. I'm trying to solve a murder," Audrey shot back.

Ben smiled when she called him Sheriff. "You know we're all after the same thing…the killer. My notion is that if we pool our resources, things might happen."

"And what resources would that be?" Audrey asked.

"I have experience working a murder case." Ben said as he thought back to the murder of a young woman in Winchester, Tennessee. He omitted the fact that it was his first and only murder case.

"Thanks, but no thanks, Sheriff. Detective Anderson and I are assigned this investigation and right now it seems like things might begin to happen. We don't need your help. We work alone," Audrey shot back.

Ben flashed his wide grin and stood up. "Whatever sails your boat, little lady."

"And don't call me little lady," Audrey said.

Ben smiled, "You're the darnedest female I ever saw… 'cept for one. Her name's Penny. She's the secretary back in my office in Franklin County Tennessee. She chews me up and spits me out couple of times a day. Didn't know how much I missed the experience until tonight. Makes me feel down right homesick."

Ben walked away as he chuckled and shook his head.

Chapter 19

Matt followed his torch beam, and ascended the unlit stairs cautiously. When he reached the top step, he turned left. The cavernous corridor of the west wing lay before him like a dark abyss. He found it suddenly strange and intimidating. He wished that he had stayed at his old home place. Although not as grand as Berryhill, the old home place felt secure and familiar, and he could get around in the dark without stumbling. He passed Steve's door and then Einer's. He didn't hear a sound from either room. When he reached Peedee's room, he thought he heard a faint rustle as if someone were pacing back and forth. Finally he reached the end of the hall. As a point of location, the door to his room was located beside a third flight of stairs that led up to the ballroom. Fumbling about he found the knob and opened the door. He shuddered as a cold gust of air brushed his face.

Matt saw no reason to undress. Too many things could happen during a hurricane that require immediate action. So he stretched out on the bed and let his thoughts drift back to other hurricanes in other times. When Matt was young, the report of a mere tropical storm incited Steve and him to plot daring, foolish feats. By the time the storm was upgraded to a hurricane, their plots were hatched. The excitement grew as the hurricane approached. If they were on the Outer Banks when the hurricane hit, they took unbelievable risks on the beach. Only young men who had not yet come to terms with their own mortality would perform such daring and foolish acts. And then there were the hurricane parties with kegs of beer and lots of beach music. They invited anyone looking for a good time. Sometimes they'd invite tourists who marveled at their defiance of nature. Once Steve perched upon the roof of the cottage. He stood with arms outstretched facing the ocean and yelling, "Odin, Odin" in a summons to the Norse God of wind.

These hurricanes soirees always included Margot, Annie-Ann, Noah, and of course, Caryn. Caryn, yes Caryn. How many times he'd thought of her since returning to Virginia. She was an important part of his memories here. Caryn was memories of footprints on the beach, boogie boarding in the surf, and unsuccessful hang gliding attempts. She was memories of bond fires, sand castles, and forbidden late night swims. Caryn had honey-colored hair that framed her oval-shaped, porcelain face. And she had piercing jade eyes. Smiling eyes that encouraged and reassured.

And when Matt was a young man, he needed reassurance. His college years were somber, violent, and desperate times in this country. The quagmire in Vietnam appeared to be sacrificing not only the young men but also the country's character. Riots and demonstrations were the order of the day.

Matt detested upheaval, so he'd flee to the remote Outer Banks. They would all go down…Annie-Ann, Margot, Noah, Steve, and Caryn. They'd pile into the old gray Lincoln that his dad passed down to Steve and him and escape to the seclusion of the beach. Tonight Matt felt that same desire to escape. Escape the grief of Noah's death and Aunt Peedee's crazy obsession with the paranormal.

Escape the knowledge of Einer's affair with Mary and his relationship to Noah. Escape the prying questions of those detectives who kept popping in. And escape this damned hurricane that threatened to flood the entire peninsula.

Matt thought how comforting it would be to talk with Caryn again. He promised himself that he would call her as soon as this storm passed.

So Matt lay on his bed and listened as the house groaned under the pressure of the torrential rain. He slept intermittently. Dispersed within these brief periods of sleep were dreams of primeval marshlands in which Noah appeared grinning and beckoning to Matt. Matt felt a rush of happiness and walked toward him only to see him vanish into the mist. Other dreams were even more unsettling. Matt saw the boggy river bottom teeming with carnivorous crabs. They writhed and squirmed as they searched the river floor for something to satisfy their prehistoric instinct as scavengers.

House sounds roused Matt from the dreams. Limbs scrapped against the windows. A loosened shudder flapped against the house somewhere in the distance. Drafts of wind entered through ancient cracks and crevices and swept down the hall making uncanny sounds.

Matt replayed the events of the day in his mind. The new information they'd learned about Einer and Noah served only to raise more questions and contribute to his sleeplessness.

* * *

Ben stood with his ear to Ignatius' door. He rapped softly.

"You still up?" he whispered.

"Who?" Ignatius asked.

"It's me. Ben."

"Come on in. Door's unlocked."

Ben opened the door and came in. Pete still cowered in Ignatius's lap. Ignatius stoked the small fire that smoldered in the fireplace.

"I don't think we oughta have fires in these fireplaces with all that wind kicking up," he said. "But this is my first hurricane, so who am I to say?"

"I don't know, 'Natius, seems to me that you should have as much say as anyone…."

Ignatius cut him off. "The question was rhetorical, Ben. You didn't have to answer it."

Ben grinned, "Sorry I answered your rhetorical question, 'Natius," he said waggishly. "but if you got a minute, like to bounce a few things around."

Ignatius placed the poker by the fireplace and began to stroke Pete. "Shoot," he said.

"I can't seem to think of a suspect in this house who has all the big three elements…motive, means and opportunity," Ben said.

"You taking over this investigation?" Ignatius asked.

"No, but don't expect me not to be curious. Hell, I am a Sheriff. What Sheriff wouldn't be curious if he was flopped right down in the middle of a murder?" Ben justified. Then he added roguishly, "You don't have to answer that. It's a rhetorical question."

Ignatius frowned displaying his usual intolerance for humor. "Okay, I'll play your game. Let's start with ladies first. What about Carrie?"

"Nope. There could be an unknown motive, but both she and Steve were in Portsmouth at the time Noah went missing."

Ignatius lit his pipe creating billows of smoke. "Margot?"

"Again, could be some kind of family motive we don't know about, and she had opportunity. I heard her say that she took Noah for boat rides, so Margot knows how to drive a boat. She could have followed him out that morning. But, I don't think she's strong enough to reach from one boat to another and bludgeon him to death."

"What about Peedee, the nincompoop? I wouldn't put anything past her."

"Now I wish you wouldn't come down so hard on Miz Peedee, 'Natius. She's a fine lady. What you got against her anyway?"

"I just don't hold with all this paranormal claptrap. Poor Carrie's almost hysterical. Peedee should have more regard for other people's feelings."

"Did you ever stop to think that it might not be claptrap to her?" Ben argued. Then he stopped abruptly. "We've got off the subject here. Again Miz Peedee could have a family-related motive, but there's no way she could follow him in a boat. Why I doubt she could get into one of those boats unassisted. Anyway she certainly couldn't bludgeon Big Noah. So based on what we know now, that lets all the women off the hook... for the time being anyway. I think this killer was a man."

180

Ignatius nodded. "I think you're right. It took a man to commit this murder. And I think he was a big man, and someone Noah knew."

"'Xactly what I think," Ben agreed.

The logs burned low, and the embers glowed in a futile attempt to ignite a flame. Ignatius drew heavily on his pipe and watched the fire sputter. "Alright, let's talk about the men."

"Now that's the troubling thing," said Ben. "You, Matt, and me weren't even here when Noah disappeared. So those detectives out there," he jabbed a thumb in the direction of the library, "are barking up the wrong tree calling Winchester and trying to connect us in any way. Steve, of course, was still in Portsmouth. So that just leaves Einer."

Ignatius' face took on a troubled expression. He simply nodded.

Ben continued, "Einer had the means. Those powerboats are his, and he knew how to operate them. Told me so when he offered to take us fishing. He could easily have followed Noah onto the river. He's a big, strong fellow, too. Quite capable of performing the act."

"Yeah, when he's not drinking," added Ignatius.

Ben continued doggedly, "I don't think he'd have any trouble overpowering Noah. 'Natius, it pains me to say this about our gracious host, but if I were those two detectives out there, I'd be thinking that Einer is the most likely suspect."

"Huh," grunted Ignatius. "But you still got one important thing missing, Ben."

"Yeah?"

"Motive."

"That's what I see missing, too 'Natius. All this stuff 'bout Einer being Noah's father...so what? That's no motive. Einer's had years to kill Noah if he wanted to, and he's smart enough and rich enough to get it done in a way as not to leave a trail back to him. And if he was afraid somebody was gonna find out he was a father, I can't see Noah as a likely one to let the cat out of the bag. How would he know who his natural father is? And if he did and if he told it, no one would believe him."

"You'll get no argument from me on that," Ignatius said. "But who is the low-life that wrote that letter, and what's *his* motive?"

"'Natius, you've hit the nail on the head. If we find out who wrote that letter then we might find ourselves a killer," Ben said enthusiastically.

"We? Where do you come off with this *we* stuff?" Ignatius asked. "Ben, there's two police detectives our there chomping at the bit to put the first notch on their arrest belt, and they are not going to take kindly to any help from you...no matter how well intended. So before your lady friend puts you in your place again, I'd advise you to just back off."

"'Natius," Ben drawled and beamed, "if I got to be put in my place, I can't think of anyone I'd rather have do it than Miss Audrey."

* * *

Audrey squirmed about in an effort to relieve her aching muscles. After several restless hours the over-stuffed chair proved not to be as comfortable as it appeared. Her face and hands were covered with scratches inflicted by swirling shredded leaves and splinters from branches. The jagged cuts itched as the heat from the fire dried the wounds. Her hair was a tangled, matted mess, and she ached all over. She pulled at the housedress that Margot found for her to replace her wet uniform. It was at least one size too small, and it bound her shoulders that were already throbbing from the tension of her ordeal. She sat up and looked irritably across at Donald slouched in his chair and snoring peacefully. She gave his foot a kick.

"Donald," she snarled. "Wake up. You want to wake up the whole house?"

Donald snapped awake. He sat upright and looked bewildered. His eyes darted about the room as he struggled to remember where he was and recall what brought him here.

"What?" he said in a dazed voice. "Oh no. I wish this were a dream. The Chief is gonna handcuff us to a desk and throw away the key. I can't believe we did this."

"Well believe it, Donald," said Audrey. She rubbed her neck and stretched her arms upward. "I've never been so cold and stiff in my whole life."

"Audrey, I wish you hadn't been so hard on Sheriff Day. He seems to be a nice enough guy, and he is a sheriff, for God's sake. I think you're letting your personal feelings interfere with your professional judgement. What's wrong with taking him on board for this investigation…at least while we're here at Berryhill? I think it's your pride. You're too damned stubborn and proud to accept help, especially from Sheriff Day, and that could cost us the case."

Donald had never spoken so candidly with Audrey. She was shocked. After a few silent minutes she said contritely, "Donald, do you really think I'm been too rude? You know I wouldn't intentionally damage this case for anything."

Donald replied more sympathetically this time, "I know you wouldn't damage the case intentionally, Audrey. I just sense this personal thing between you and Sheriff Day, and I think you should be aware of it when you make decisions."

Audrey stood up and examined her boots that had been drying by the fire. She felt inside and discovered that they were still wet. Her gun lay on the floor beside the chair and her slacks were spread out upon the hearth.

"Why didn't you borrow some clothes and let your uniform dry?" Audrey asked, steering the conversation to something mundane.

"I just don't like to wear other people's things."

Audrey sighed and settled her smarting body back into the soft stuffed chair. She lifted her feet onto the ottoman, and laid her head back. Outside the rain pelted the windowpanes like an intruder threatening to invade their sanctuary. She listened to the mournful cry of the wind like a child lost somewhere in the house. But as she listened, she began aware of something else. It was a curious sound. At first she couldn't tell if it were inside or outside of the house. It was far away. It sounded like hesitant footsteps that occasionally bumped against things.

Audrey nudged Donald and placed a finger over her lips, signaling him to be quiet. Donald froze, lifted his head and strained to listen. Suddenly his eyes opened widely, and he nodded indicating that he too heard the noise.

The two detectives crept softly to the library door. It stood slightly ajar. They quietly pushed it open and stepped into the grand entrance hall. They didn't use their flashlights but moved cautiously along in the darkness. They had left their boots by the fireplace, so their footsteps were inaudible. Suddenly, Audrey felt a hand gently tap her shoulder. She froze. Ben stepped in front of her, his lips pursed in a silent shhh. He pointed toward the dark staircase. At that moment, a door opened somewhere upstairs and a rushing draft blew through the hallway and down the stairwell. The door to the library blew shut with a bang.

Suddenly a light appeared at the west end of the upstairs balcony. Ben darted for the staircase. He missed the first step and fell. When he regained footing he looked up the staircase just as Peedee appeared on the balcony, a candle in her hand.

"Who's there? Noah is that you?" she asked falteringly.

At that moment, a dark figure stepped from the shadows and knocked the candle from her hand. There was a clatter as the candle and holder hit the floor, plunging them all into darkness. Peedee's shrieks filled the long corridor and resonated through the house.

From downstairs someone cast a beam of light upward and illuminated the upstairs balcony. Peedee was struggling with someone. An unidentifiable dark figure shoved her towards the railing. She grasped the balustrade desperately. The figure grappled with her trying to loosen her hold, but Peedee held on for dear life, her screams reverberating through the halls.

Ben raced up the steps yelling, "Let her go. Let her go."

The dark figure turned and looked toward Ben, and with one last hard shove pushed Peedee against the railing. She lost her balance and teetered precariously over the edge. Ben reached the upstairs balcony just in time to grab her and prevent her plummeting into the hall below. She grasped Ben desperately. As Ben consoled Peedee, he saw the attacker disappear into the darkness of the east corridor.

Peedee was hysterical. Her cries and shrieks echoed through the house. Audrey and Donald flew up the stairs, and from below Ignatius' voice called, "Ben is everyone alright up there?"

"Everyone here is okay 'Natius. Miz Peedee's scared out of her wits through," he replied all the time patting and comforting Peedee who clung to him frantically.

"See who that was?" Ignatius asked.

"No, I was more concerned about Miz Peedee," he said. "But don't you worry, that scoundrel ain't going no where…not tonight."

The uproar roused the others, and the sound of opening doors could be heard in the dark hallway. Beams of light followed the sounds, and Matt, Margot, Carrie and Steve emerged from the west corridor.

There was an explosion of questions, and Audrey gently escorted a terrified Peedee down the stairs and towards the library.

Hoping to answer all questions with one explanation, Ben said in a loud voice, "Some one tried to kill Miz Peedee." There was instant silence.

186

Matt spoke first, "Who was it? Where did he go?"

Ben said, "I don't know who it was, but I know where he went. Come on Matt, Steve."

Ben darted across the balcony and headed toward the east corridor. Steve and Matt followed close behind. Then a figure suddenly appeared from the shadows of the east corridor, and Einer stepped forth. He demanded, "What the hell's going on?"

Chapter 20

Concerned for Peedee, who was still hysterical, everyone gathered in the library. Margot and Carrie struggled to calm their aunt while Matt, Ignatius, Steve, and Ben talked at once. Audrey and Donald watched the commotion in amazement unsure of their authority and what their next move should be.

Einer calmly walked to the bar and poured himself a hefty drink. He took several gulps and turned to the group. In a commanding voice he said, "Alright, let's talk about it." Einer assumed control even though his entry from the east corridor cast him as prime suspect for Peedee's attack.

The room fell silent. No one wanted to ask Einer why he was in the east wing of his own home. Matt fidgeted nervously, and Ignatius chomped the stem of his pipe mercilessly. Ben was calm and remained silent.

Einer walked slowly to the fireplace and turned to face his family and guests. "Ben, why don't you start us off," he said, dismissing the presence of the two local law enforcement officers.

Not surprisingly, Ben consented. "Alright, Einer, if you really want me to. I was over in 'Natius' room talking to him when I heard a thump. Sounded like it came from upstairs. I slipped out of 'Natius's room and into the hallway. There I saw Detectives Kelly and Anderson creeping toward the stairway. I motioned to them and the three of us started up."

He turned to Audrey. "Detective Kelly. Tell us why you were in the hall."

Audrey shrugged, "The same reason you were. Donald and I heard a noise and what sounded like stumbling footsteps. We were going to check it out. I…we thought that a family member would have no reason to sneak around like that."

"Makes sense to me," Ben agreed. "Is that your reason for being out there too, Detective Anderson?"

Donald merely said, "Yes." He was impressed by Ben's performance.

Ben continued, "Now just as the three of us started up the steps real good, Miz Peedee comes out on the balcony holding a candle. Miz Peedee, want to tell us why you were out there in the middle of the night."

Einer interrupted, "And why the hell were you carrying a candle? Want to burn the house down? Why do you think I passed out those flashlights?"

"Einer, please." It was Margot, and she embraced Peedee comfortingly.

Ben repeated the question, "Could you tell us why you were out there Miz Peedee?"

Peedee straightened and held her head up confidently. "I heard a rustling in the hallway. It sounded liked footsteps. I went to see if Noah's spirit had indeed returned to help us catch his murderer. I even called to him. That was just before…before…" Peedee burst into tears.

"That's alright, Miz Peedee. We know what happened next," Ben said comfortingly. "Could you tell us where the attacker came from?"

"Well, I'm not positive," she said hesitatingly, "but I think it came from the east wing of the house. I can't be certain. You see, it was a terrifying thing. Just terrifying," Peedee collapsed into tears again.

"Thank you, Miz Peedee," Ben said gently. He turned to Einer and said, "Now Einer, can you tell us what you were doing in the east wing of the house in the middle of the night?"

Einer looked squarely at Ben and said unwaveringly, "Be glad to, Ben. I had difficulty sleeping. I heard what I considered to be several suspicious noises. I disregarded them, thinking that they were resulting from the hurricane. Then I heard a sound that was different. That noise was not just a trick of nature. It sounded like footsteps somewhere in the east wing of the house. I went to investigate and ended up at the fartherest end of the corridor. When I heard Peedee's screams, I rushed to the balcony to find …well, you were there. You know what I found."

"Did you find anyone when you went to investigate?"

"No."

"You see anyone run pass you in that corridor?"

"No."

 "Hear any doors close?"

"No."

"Hear any noises in any of the other rooms in the east wing?"

"No."

"Did you go in any of the rooms?"

"No, I returned to the balcony as soon as I heard Peedee scream."

"Einer," said Ben incredulously, "do you mean to tell us that you went to the east wing to check on a suspicious noise and you just checked the hall, and didn't check the rooms?"

"You don't know how many rooms there are in that wing, Ben. I don't even know myself..."

"Ben, he's right," it was Margot, her voice defensive. "The east wing was built years after the original house. The family doesn't use it. It's used mainly for retreats, conferences, accommodations for Einer's business associates. There are a number of bedrooms, several sitting rooms, and a conference room. It's really like a second house attached to this original structure. The rooms are closed off and the furniture covered when the wing is not in use. It would be impossible for Einer to search all those rooms in the middle of the night with just a flashlight." Her voice was becoming loud and shrill.

Einer walked to Margot. "Margot, it's alright. Don't get upset." He pulled her to him. "Ben understands now. Don't you, Ben?"

Margot began to cry, and everyone talked at once. The inquiry was again reduced to bedlam.

Suddenly from the back of the room Peedee screeched, "Stop it. I want you all to stop it right now. You're behaving as if Einer were the attacker. You seem to be accusing Einer of trying to push me over the railing. That's wrong. I know it's wrong. It was not Einer. It couldn't be."

All eyes turned to Peedee. Ben walked over to her and gently took her by the shoulders. He said, "Miz Peedee, how can you be sure? How can you be certain that the attacker was not Einer?" he asked.

Peedee shrugged from his grip and turned to face her audience. "Because," she stated simply, "He...the attacker was not as... as..."

"Yes?" prompted Ben. "He was not what?"

"He was not as *portly* as Einer," she said emphatically.

Chapter 21

The decision was made to search the house. Ben organized the search. Einer described the floor plan of the area to be searched. The east wing was a maze of hallways with many bedrooms and sitting rooms. Some were located at the end of small staircases in order to provide privacy for guests. Each bedroom had double closets and a bathroom. At the end of the wing was a conference room equipped with a large table and numerous cabinets and closets. Furniture was covered with white dust clothes when the wing was not in use. At the farthest end of the wing was a staircase leading to the third floor of the original structure. This staircase mirrored the one found in the west wing beside Matt's room. Einer explained that a massive ballroom comprised the entire third floor and contained several closets and cabinets and a mahogany bar that ran the width of the room.

The guests were amazed at the description of the east wing and the size of the area that they would search. "Sounds like a hotel," exclaimed Ignatius.

"In a sense, it is," said Einer. "I find it's simpler to have my business associates stay here rather than in town."

"Well, we need to get started. Steve, you know that part of the house?" Ben asked.

"Pretty well," said Steve. "Carrie and I have wandered through it several times."

"Matt, do you know that wing?"

"No, until now, I've just made short visits to Berryhill," Matt replied.

"Okay, then. Matt, you and Steve go together. Take the left side of the main corridor. Einer, you be my guide. We'll take the right side of the main corridor. Check every room, under furniture, in closets and bathrooms. When we get through searching each side, we'll meet at the conference room before heading upstairs to the ballroom."

Margot moved to Einer. "Einer, please don't go up there. We have two policemen here, plus Sheriff Day. They are trained for this kind of assignment. Stay here, Einer, please."

Einer drew Margot to him. "Now don't you worry about a thing, dear. These men don't know the house, and you know how confusing that east wing can be. I know the floor plan, and I'll guide them. Don't worry. We'll be alright."

"Hey, what about us?" It was Audrey.

Ben said, "I was thinking that one of you officers should stay with Miz Peedee since an attempt was made on her life tonight. The other could be my *companion*." Ben beamed with anticipation. "Who'll it be Detective Kelly?"

Audrey looked disgusted. "I'll *accompany* you, Sheriff. I just wish I were wearing my uniform instead of this dress."

"'Natius, you assist Detective Anderson. Detective, you got your gun." It was a statement not a question.

"Yes, sir," Donald slapped his sidearm.

"Well, don't be afraid to use it if you need to, but just be damned sure of what you're shooting at," said Ben.

"Yes, sir."

"Now if you all will hold up a minute. Be right back."

Ben rushed out of the library and into his room. He found his canvas bag and began to toss the contents onto the bed. At the bottom of the bag he found what he was looking for. Ben pulled out a holster containing a Colt .38 special revolver.

"Sure hadn't planned to use this on my vacation," Ben said.

* * *

The searchers ascended the grand stairway and stepped onto the balcony. They made their way to the east wing, and began the search. Matt and Steve took the left side of the main corridor, and Einer led Ben and Audrey down the right side. In the darkness, the corridor seemed endless. It branched into other smaller hallways and up short flights of steps to rooms and more hallways. Pictures displayed in antique frames hung on the walls of the corridor. Mostly they were old pictures of people from another era.

"Ancestors," Einer explained simply.

All the doors were closed. Ben reached for a door handle and turned it. It was locked. Einer removed a key from his pocket and inserted it into the keyhole. "This key fits them all. I gave one to Steve, too," he said.

They pushed the door, and stepped into a large bedroom. Pictures of landscapes and portraits similar to those found in the hall adorned the wall of the room.

Windows held leaded stain glass that obscured the rain that beat against the panes. The furniture was covered with thick white dust covers. Ben and Einer lifted every cover and shined their flashlights underneath. Audrey dropped to her knees and looked under the bed.

They entered more rooms using the same search procedure. Audrey was in awe of the elaborate hanging tapestries and embroidered velvet pillows. There were elegant pieces of furniture and unusual curios in every room. Bookshelves held books bound in leather, and fireplaces stood ready to be lit at a moment's notice. Rugs beautifully seasoned by years of wear adorned the shining floors, and in each room portraits of Pellinger ancestors stared disapprovingly at the intrusion.

In another part of the east wing, Matt and Steve slowly searched one room after another. They, too, gawked at the opulence. Several times they became disoriented after turning down a dead end hallway. They were obliged to retrace their steps in order to get back on course.

Rain pounded the windows and roof mercilessly, and the wind sounded like it was inside the house, not outside. Sometimes the wind made haunting, hopeless sounds like some poor soul grieving for lost loves or missed opportunities.

"Did you hear that?" Matt whispered. "I thought I heard footsteps."

"No," answered Steve. "It's the wind. It makes all sorts of noises when it gets into an old house like this"

Having searched their assigned portion of the wing, Matt and Steve made their way toward the conference room. The main corridor seemed longer, darker, and unfamiliar.

"Are you sure we're going the right way?" asked Matt.

"No, I'm not sure, but I believe this looks right," said Steve.

They thought they remembered the short hallway with a landscape watercolor of a misty English countryside, so they followed their dimming flashlight beam through that hall and down a short staircase. They should turn right...or was it left?

"All we need is for the damned flashlight to go out on us," said Steve. "We'd never find the conference room then."

Finally, much to their relief, Steve and Matt saw a faint glow ahead. They hurried in that direction. Soon they were standing inside the conference room.

"Anything?" asked Ben.

"Not a thing. We gave it a real good look too," said Matt.

"Well, that just leaves one place for our friend to be. He's got to be up in the ballroom," said Ben. "You know, we don't know who we're dealing with. We don't know if he is armed or crazy or what. Now Einer, Matt, Steve, I suggest you give a lot of thought about continuing this pursuit. You ain't trained for this. Since we've narrowed down his hiding place to one room Miz...uh Detective Kelly and I can handle it from here on."

They all looked at Einer. He was seated at the conference table, handkerchief in hand. Perspiration rolled profusely down his face and neck. His shirt was wet, and he was breathing heavily.

"He's right, Mr. Pellinger. Now that we know the layout of the place, the Sheriff and I will find him," said

Audrey, surprised that she would agree so readily with Ben. And she had called him Sheriff.

Einer took several deep breaths and eyed the other members of the search party. He wiped his face and said hoarsely, "Someone violated my home tonight. They terrorized my wife and guests and tried to murder a dear friend. He may have murdered Noah. I feel an obligation to defend my home, and I personally intend to help find this scum. And when I do, I'll see that he's punished to the full extent of the law." He shook his fist and reiterated, "The fullest extent of the law!"

Ben reached over and slapped Einer on the shoulder. "I got you, Buddy. Now let's talk about how we're gonna do this."

Realizing that there were two entrances to the third floor ballroom, the decision was made for Matt and Steve to return to the west wing of the house and enter the ballroom by the west staircase. Audrey, Ben, and Einer would enter by the east staircase.

"Do you think you can find your way back to the balcony without getting lost?" Einer asked. "It's so damned dark, and the corridor can be confusing."

"I don't think we'll have any problems," said Steve.

"Remember, just stick to the main corridor. As long as you don't get off on any of the side hallways you'll be okay," Einer reminded them.

"Okay," said Ben focusing his flashlight on his watch, "we'll wait fifteen minutes and start up the steps. Matt, got your watch?"

"Right, fifteen minutes," said Matt checking the time.

"Remember, we don't know nothing about this person," Ben reminded them. "He could be armed, and he could be just plain crazy. At any rate, don't take no chances."

Matt and Steve nodded and started back down the long dark corridor in the direction of the west wing. Returning to the balcony was much simpler than the search that required them to veer off the main passage.

In the meantime, Audrey and Ben waited silently. The fifteen minute wait gave Einer a chance to catch his breath. Soon his breathing was easier, and Audrey and Ben relaxed. Audrey could not help wondering what the Chief would say if Einer Pellinger had a heart attack while assisting in a police search of Berryhill.

Ben looked at his watch. "Okay, it's time," he said. "Let's move on to the third-floor stairway."

They used just one flashlight as they made their way up the unlit stairwell to the ballroom. Audrey unsnapped the leather strap that secured her gun and shifted her holster.

"Be careful now. Remember, Matt and Steve will be entering the ballroom from the other end," Ben cautioned her. She nodded.

"Let me go first," Ben said. "And try to be as quiet as you can."

Ben removed the .38 from his holster and stared anxiously into the darkness ahead of them. A draft swept by them as they climbed the steps, and with each step, the creaking boards whispered warnings of danger at the top of the stairs.

With his gun pointed upward, Ben reached the top of the stairs and stepped into the ballroom. He clicked on his flashlight. At the other end of the room, another light responded as Matt and Steve signaled that they too had reached the third floor. Two flashlight beams swept the ballroom. The room was void of furniture except for a row of Windsor chairs resting neatly against a mahogany chair rail that ran along one side of the room. Closet doors extended along the opposite side of the room. A large brass-trimmed mahogany bar was located by the top of the staircase and stretched the width of the east wall. Enormous skylights were set into the ceiling, and branches and rotting leaves stuck to the glass. Audrey thought how romantic it would be to dance in this ballroom on a clear, starry night.

Her momentary fantasy was interrupted when Ben nudged her arm. He motioned for her to check behind the bar, and signaled Einer to come with him to search the closets along the side of the room.

Matt and Steve observed the movement of the light beams at the other end of the room and began to check the closets from the west end. Click, slam, click, slam. The menacing noise echoed through the room as the men opened and closed each closet door.

Meantime, Audrey checked behind the bar. She flashed her light along the deserted floor. Behind the bar were large cabinets for liquor and glassware storage. She concluded the cabinets were large enough to conceal a desperate person, so she began to check each one. She opened and closed each cabinet door making her way down the length of the bar. She had not gone far when her dress became tangled with something under the bar. She gave it a tug in an effort to loosen it. Damn, it was still snagged. She gave it another yank…then another. Then suddenly it jerked back. Audrey squealed. The dress was held firmly.

"Audrey, what is it?" Ben's voice thundered through the room followed by rapid footsteps.

Her dress was held taunt, and a quavering voice from beneath the bar whimpered, "Margot, Margot, please help me, please help me."

Summoning her courage, Audrey knelt and shined her flashlight under the bar and into a pair of bulging terrified eyes. Ben and Einer quickly joined her. Ben bent down and peered under the bar.

"Who the hell?" exclaimed Ben.

Einer spoke in a raspy voice, "Ben, Detective Kelly, let me introduce my father-in-law, Wilson Delamar."

Einer and Ben were pulling Wilson from under the bar when Matt and Steve ran up.

"Wilson," they said stunned.

Wilson was shaking and crying, his hands covering his face. For a few moments, Matt felt sorry for the pathetic man. Then Wilson removed his hands from his eyes, and he suddenly stopped crying and trembling. He stared at Audrey in disbelief, and a look of shock covered his face. Then suddenly in anger, he wrestled from Ben's grasp and went for Audrey. He lunged for her neck, spittle drooling down his chin. His babbling was almost unintelligible.

"You're not Margot, you bitch. You're not my daughter. That dress...how dare you impersonate my daughter! I'll kill you...kill you..." Wilson howled.

It took the four men and Audrey to overpower him. Then after a few minutes of savage struggle, Wilson sank to the floor. Audrey handcuffed him and fell back on the bar, gasping for breath.

Ben reached for Audrey and drew her to him, stroking her matted hair. "You did real good, Little Lady," he said soothingly. "Real good."

Audrey didn't pull away, but clung to him desperately. She didn't mind that he called her Little Lady instead of Detective Kelly. She didn't mind at all, and she felt surprisingly warm and safe in his arms.

Chapter 22

After Wilson Delamar was handcuffed, he lapsed into a catatonic stupor. The immediate crisis having been resolved, Einer's thoughts now turned to Margot. How would she react when she learned that her father tried to kill Peedee and probably killed Noah? He suggested holding Wilson in the conference room until he could break the news to her. Matt, Steve, and Ben practically carried Wilson Delamar from the third floor ballroom to the conference room. Audrey used two flashlights to illuminate the dark stairs and hallway for them. When they got Wilson to the conference room, they were unable to manipulate his limbs, so they simply propped him in a corner of the room where he sat unblinking into the darkness.

"Ben might I make a suggestion?" asked Einer.

"Sure, Einer. It's your game." Ben was surprised. It was unlike Einer to ask permission to do anything, but Einer had entrusted the search to Ben and that decision proved to be a wise one. So he decided that Ben remain in charge until help arrived.

"Ben, as I said, I'm concerned for Margot. I'd like to tell her privately that her father is the one who tried to kill Peedee. Even though Margot has come to terms with Wilson's worthlessness, I don't think she ever considered him capable of murder," said Einer.

"I understand what you're saying," said Ben. "I think that's a good idea."

"How do you want to work this?" asked Einer

"Let's see, Steve, you go down and tell the others that everything is under control, and that we're going to hold the intruder up here in the conference room. Don't say who he is. Then have Donald call the police station and get some help up here right away. After Donald makes the call, he can come to the ballroom and relieve Matt and Einer. Then Einer, you can take Margot aside and talk to her. Matt, you and Steve can fill the others in."

"Sounds like a plan," said Steve. "I'm on it." And he disappeared down the hall.

* * *

Donald made a third try at reaching the James City Police Station. Finally a connect.

"James City County Police," a tired voice said.

"This is Detective Anderson at Berryhill Estate. I'm trying to locate the Chief. He around?"

"Anderson...the chief's been yelling for you and Kelly for hours. You hold on."

Donald waited anxiously. It wasn't good news that the Chief was unable to raise the two detectives when he needed them. Donald prepared for another upbraiding. It seemed like he and his partner couldn't do anything to please their Chief.

His fear was confirmed when an angry voice shouted through the phone, "Anderson, where the hell are you? I been trying to reach you all night. Is Kelly with you?"

"Yes, sir, Kelly is with me. And we are a Berryhill Estate, we…."

"What? Berryhill Estate? What the hell are you doing…?"

"Sir, we were summonsed. An emergency thing. Took us forever to get here and when…"

"Anderson, who summonsed you? Was it Einer Pellinger?"

"No, sir. It was Mrs. Peedee Murray. Although we didn't know that at…"

"Mrs. Peedee Murray?" the Chief yelled. Peedee's eccentric reputation was well known throughout the county. "Detective, did you check with Pellinger before showing up?"

"Uh…we thought about it, Sir, but decided that if we did, we'd lose the element of surprise."

"Element of surprise?" the Chief repeated sarcastically. "Anderson, if you have not already created a mess that will land me in early retirement, you better get your ass back to this station even if you have to swim…"

"But Chief, we can't leave now," Donald interrupted anxiously.

"Detective, you've got more to worry about than this hurricane. You've got your whole damned career out there to think of," the Chief threatened.

"I know, Chief," Donald said apprehensively. "But it's not the hurricane that's got us stuck here. It's this crazy intruder. He tried to kill Mrs. Peedee."

"What? What intruder? Is Peedee Murray alright? Is Einer Pellinger alright? What about Mrs. Pellinger? Speak up, man," the Chief yelled.

"That's what I'm trying to tell you, Chief. An intruder broke in and tried to push Mrs. Murray off the upstairs balcony. Mr. Pellinger is all right and so is everyone else. That Sheriff from Tennessee and Audrey took some of the men on a search of the house. They found the guy. Problem is we don't know what to do with him. We sure can't bring him in this storm, so we're just holding him in the conference room upstairs."

"I'll tell you what to do with him, Anderson. You get on up there with Kelly and you two sit on that guy until I get out there. Don't move. Just wait…by the way, who is he?"

"Don't know, Chief. Mr. Harder and I stayed downstairs to cover Mrs. Pellinger and Mrs. Murray while the others searched. A few minutes ago, Sheriff Day sent one of Mrs. Pellinger's cousins down and said I should call you and then come on upstairs. He wouldn't say who the attacker is."

"Oh geez, he's taking orders from a cousin and a Tennessee Sheriff," muttered the Chief.

"What's that Chief?"

"Nothing. Just sit tight until I get there."

"Right."

The Chief pushed himself away from his desk and rushed to his office door. His eyes scanned the near empty reception room. Then he spotted a weary, soaking wet patrol officer.

"Harvey, we need to get out to Berryhill Estates right away. What's Route Five like?"

"No way, Chief. There are trees across the road at several points, and the road is washed over in a lot of

206

places. It's going to be a long time before anybody can get down that road."

"Can't wait, Harvey. Got an emergency. Call the county road services, call the highway patrol, call anybody who can give us an alternate route to Berryhill. I don't care how circuitous it is."

Harvey looked stunned. *"Now*, Harvey, call them *now,"* the Chief yelled.

* * *

"Steve, please tell us," begged Carrie. "Do you know who the intruder is?"

"Carrie, just wait. Einer and Matt will be down in a few minutes, and they'll fill you in on everything." He nodded toward Margot and frowned.

Margot was occupied with comforting Peedee. Coping with Noah's death, the murder investigation, and now an intruder left both women near the breaking point.

Ignatius looked out the window. The first light of morning filtered through the curtains of rain. The wind blew relentlessly, and Pete shivered in his master's arms.

"This dog hasn't had a pee in ten hours. He's going to have a ruptured bladder. Since things are secured now, I think I'll try to get him to use one of the poop pads Margot gave me. Tell Matt and Einer to wait on the reporting until I get back in here." He turned his wheel chair and headed towards the hall and his room.

* * *

207

Einer and Matt descended the stairs slowly. "I'd give anything if I didn't have to tell Margot about that bastard," said Einer. "He's hurt her enough."

"I certainly don't envy you," Matt replied sympathetically.

As they entered the library, Margot rushed to Einer. She clung to him desperately without speaking. He murmured comforting words to her and steered her across the hall and into the parlor. A match struck, a candle flickered, and then the parlor door closed quietly.

"Now, Steve," said Carrie. "Tell us what's going on."

"Wait for Ignatius," he said.

"You don't have to wait. I'm here." It was Ignatius wheeling through the door, with a much-relieved Pete in tow.

"Einer is explaining things to Margot privately. Matt, you want to tell them, or me?" asked Steve.

"We both can, but Aunt Peedee please sit down," said Matt.

"I wish people would stop fussing over me and telling me to sit down. I don't want to sit, Matt. I want to know who tried to kill me," Peedee replied impatiently.

"Aunt Peedee, the intruder who tried to push you over the balcony was Wilson Delamar," Matt said bluntly.

"What?" exclaimed Carrie. "I can't believe it. Are you sure?"

"Sure as rain, Carrie," said Steve.

"I can believe it," said Peedee as calmly as if someone had just announced that the day was Friday.

"He's evil, Carrie. I've always known Wilson was not to be trusted. No, I'm not surprised at all."

"For once, I have to agree with Peedee," said Ignatius. "From what Einer told us, he is a greedy, warped, self-centered person, willing to use his own flesh and blood for social and financial gain. In the vernacular, he's a son-of-a bitch."

"Describes him pretty well," said Matt. "And I'll bet you something else, too. I'll bet he killed Noah."

Anxious eyes went to Peedee, but she remained calm. She had a pensive look on her face. When she spoke, her voice was soft, composed, "I believe he killed Noah, too. And this explains the strong feeling of Noah's presence since the funeral. Now I know why Noah wouldn't go to the other side. I know why he wanted to remain here with us."

Carrie was beginning to feel apprehensive again, but curiosity prompted her to ask, "Why Aunt Peedee? Why do you think Noah's spirit remained here?"

"You see dear, Noah wasn't aroused because his killer was free, he wanted to protect Einer, Margot, and me," Peedee explained simply.

"Huh," scoffed Ignatius. Then he made his usual attempt to steer the conversation away from the paranormal and to the reality of the problem at hand. "Well, what's the motive? What reason does Wilson have to kill Peedee or Noah?"

"I don't know," said Steve. "That's for the police to find out. But what ever it is, I'll bet it has to do with money."

"I agree with you on that," said Matt.

The door to the parlor opened, and Margot and Einer walked slowly across the hall.

Margot's eyes swept the room, "Having you all here has been a life saver. I don't know what Einer and I would have done if we had been forced to go through this alone."

"Any idea when help will arrive?" asked Einer.

"Donald called the station, and the road conditions are pretty bad. There's no telling when the police can get here," said Ignatius.

"There's no reason to just sit here in the library," said Einer. "I'll have Lexie prepare some breakfast for us and send a tray up to the conference room."

"No, Einer, let me do that," said Margot. "This will give me something to do. I've felt so ineffectual tonight."

"You have never been ineffectual, my dear," Einer said earnestly.

Lexie must have anticipated her employer's request. When Margot entered the kitchen she found oil lamps lit, coffee perking, and pans of breakfast meats and pancakes sizzling on the gas stove. There was a tray on the worktable that held a variety of syrups.

"Lexie, as usual, you have everything under control," said Margot appreciatively. "Would you also prepare a tray for three people and send it up to the conference room?"

"Breakfast will be ready soon, and Travis will take the tray up to the conference room," Lexie replied.

Margot lifted the tray of syrups, "I'll just put this one in the dining room."

Margot placed the tray on the dining table and lit several candles. Although it was dawn, torrents of rain made it appear to still be nighttime. She started back to the library. When she reached the staircase, she paused and peered up the steps. She wasn't sure how long she stood there, but suddenly a hand touched her arm, and she snapped out of her dreamlike state.

"Margot, please don't. There's nothing up there for you but pain and disappointment."

Margot turned a tear-streaked face and whispered, "I know, Einer. I know."

Chapter 23

In the conference room, Ben and Audrey sat in awkward silence. Their prisoner remained in a catatonic state and offered no resistance. The only sounds were the woeful cry of the wind moving through the shattered branches of the trees and the pelting of the rain against the windowpane. Finally, the silence became unbearable.

"I…" "Ah," they spoke at once.

"I'm sorry," said Audrey.

"No, I'm sorry," stammered Ben. "Please go `head."

"I just wanted to say thank you. I'm certainly glad that you were there…behind the bar, you know. When he," she nodded toward Wilson Delamar, "grabbed me. That was really ah, ah, frightening."

"Well, you're welcome," Ben bumbled. His face was red, and he shifted nervously. He wasn't accustomed to accepting thanks from pretty young women. His conversations with women were mostly limited to bantering with his bodacious secretary, Penny.

Audrey looked away and smoothed her hair from her face. "I must look a mess." She began to straighten the dress Margot provided her. "A real mess."

"You look awfully pretty to me, little lady. I like your hair loose and free, and…," he grinned widely, "and windblown."

Audrey did not reply. She simply smiled. Ben reached for her busy hands and held them in his. Somehow, the silence was no longer awkward.

* * *

The Chief accompanied by three other officers began the dangerous drive to Berryhill. Morning light brought little help as they traveled a muddy secondary road filled with potholes and littered with tree branches. They were forced to stop several times and remove limbs from the road. Fortunately the limbs were small, and easily lifted. In several low-lying places the road was washed over, but the policemen broke a cardinal safety rule and plunged through the rushing water.

"I don't ever remember seeing this much rain in one week," commented one officer.

"If you think we have it bad, just think of those folks down in Eastern North Carolina. They've lost everything…their homes, their possessions, their animals…"

A thunderous sound drowned out their conversation, and a jolt rocked the car as a tree limb broke and crashed onto the hood of the police car.

"Okay, everybody out," said the Chief opening his door. "At this rate, we might reach Berryhill by Christmas."

* * *

Lexie did not allow a mere hurricane to compromise her breakfast. Although this meal was not as lavish as others, the diners enjoyed a variety of pancakes and syrups, several breakfast meats, and her usual superb coffee. The gloomy atmosphere certainly could not be blamed on the meal, but on the dreadful events of the previous night.

They ate in silence. Then, as they left the dining room to return to the library, streams of golden sunlight suddenly poured through the windows and bounced off the burnished wood floors. The unexpected glare caused them to squint and turn away.

"Well, what do you know," declared Ignatius. "The damned hurricane is over."

Matt looked at him almost apologetically, "I hate to disappoint you, Ignatius, but the hurricane isn't over. The eye is passing over us now."

"The eye? Explain!" Ignatius demanded.

"In the center of a hurricane is a very calm, sunny area. Strong winds and rains swirl in a circular motion around this peaceful core. The peaceful core is called the eye, and the wind and rain churning around it is the hurricane. That might be a little simplistic, but basically, that's what an eye is," explained Matt.

"So what are you telling me about the end of this hurricane? You're saying it's just half over?" Ignatius asked irritably.

"It won' be much longer, Ignatius," Einer added in an effort to be reassuring. "A lot of the rain we've had since you arrived was not part of the actual hurricane. Unfortunately, this storm was preceded by several days of rain that was just plain rain. The hurricane itself will probably be out of here by late this afternoon."

"Well, it won't be too soon for me." Ignatius said. Soon the sun disappeared and the rain and wind resumed.

"Well, here we go again," announced Steve.

* * *

When Donald entered the conference room, he sensed that Audrey's attitude toward Ben had changed greatly. The two sat side by side at the conference table, heads together and talking in whispers. They faced a man who was propped in a corner in fetal position and staring blankly into space.

Donald sat across from Ben and Audrey. "Who is he?" he asked.

"He's Margot's father, Wilson Delamar," said Ben.

"Damn!" swore Donald. "This is bizarre. You mean...why would he want to kill Mrs. Murray?"

"Don't know why," Ben said simply. "I 'spect y'all will find that out down at the police station. By the way, any luck getting through to the station?"

"Yeah," Donald said with dread apparent in his voice. "And the Chief ain't happy, Audrey. He sounded real mad."

"Big whoop, Donald. So what's new? He's been *real mad* since he put us on this case," Audrey said caustically.

Ben smiled at Audrey adoringly as if she had just made the most charming comment he'd ever heard. Donald caught his gaze, and tactfully said, "Guess I'll just move on down here closer to the prisoner."

215

Chapter 24

Einer and Margot sat silently with their guests. The pounding of the rain and the moaning of the wind had become a familiar background sound for the egregious happenings at Berryhill. They thought of all the events that moved from Peedee's demonstration of her supernatural peculiarities to the realization that Wilson Delamar was the culprit responsible for the family tragedies.

Their thoughts were interrupted by the sound of a strained car engine slowly making its way up the coach road. Einer rose.

"That would be the police," he said.

"Thank heavens. I was beginning to think they couldn't get through," said Matt.

Margot started to stand. "No, dear. I'll get the door. Wait here with the others. I want to do this by myself," Einer said as he placed a hand on Margot's shoulder.

When the sound of the car engine stopped, Einer opened the front door, and three wet and weary uniformed officers darted from the car into the house. Einer quickly closed the door. The policemen looked down apologetically as they dripped onto the rug.

"Mr. Pellinger, I'm Chief Marshall. Are you and your family okay, sir?"

"We are. Thanks in large part to Detectives Kelly and Anderson. I'll show you where the intruder is being held." The Chief looked surprised that Einer had complimented the young detectives.

Einer started towards the staircase. As they reached the bottom of the steps, Margot came out of the library. "No, dear. You stay here," he said simply and led the policemen upstairs.

Matt took Margot by the arm and led her back into the library. "Margot maybe you ought to wait until all this soaks in before you face Wilson. There's a lot to think about....."

Suddenly, the front door banged shut, and there was a commotion in the front hall. They thought another policeman had rushed in to assist the others. Then a wide-eyed, disheveled, dripping woman burst into the library. She did not resemble in the least the fastidiously dressed Aunt Dorothy who had accompanied her husband earlier to Berryhill. Her eyes darted about the room wildly.

"Margot, where's Wilson? I saw a police car. Has anything happened to him?" Her voice was shrill, earsplitting and her face reflected sheer terror.

There was a time when Margot would have been moved by Dorothy's panic. But now she realized that Dorothy's distress wasn't for the safety of someone she loved. It was for a husband she still hoped could procure for her what she wanted most---a lavish life style.

It was Peedee who stepped forward to confront Dorothy. "Dorothy, Wilson is upstairs. Einer and the policemen have gone to bring him down...."

"Bring him down? Is he hurt?"

"If you would let me finish please. No, Wilson is not hurt. He is under arrest," Peedee said with great satisfaction.

"Under arrest? What for?" Dorothy looked confused and suspicious.

"Wilson is being arrested because he tried to commit murder," Peedee said

"Murder?" Dorothy stepped forward menacingly and whispered, "You're lying you crazy old bat. Just who do you think he tried to kill?"

Ignoring the affront, Peedee stood tall, chin held high. In a regal voice, she said, "It was I that Wilson Delamar tried to kill. Last night, right here in this house before witnesses."

"Ha!" Aunt Dorothy blurted out boldly. She faced Peedee hands on her hips and a smirk on her face. "You lunatic! Everybody knows you're mad. Who do you think is going to believe a crazy old woman who goes around talking to dead people and filling my own daughter with yarns about ghosts and ghouls?"

"A lot of people!" an earsplitting voice barked from the back of the room. All eyes turned as Ignatius rolled forward to defy Aunt Dorothy.

Dorothy stared down at Ignatius contempt on her face. "And who the hell are you?"

"I, madam, am one of the witnesses to the attempt on Mrs. Peedee Murray's life. Now let me give you the names of the other eyewitnesses. There was Benjamin Day, Sheriff of Franklin County Tennessee, Police Detectives Audrey Kelly and Donald Anderson."

Dorothy was bewildered. She looked around the room at the others. Heads nodded in agreement with Ignatius. "You are lying. You are all lying..." she stammered.

Dorothy Delamar was interrupted by noises from the stairway. She rushed into the hall and saw Wilson being carried down the steps by two policemen wearing James

City County Police uniforms. He was crying and mumbling incomprehensibly.

She ran toward him, "Wilson, Wilson."

Chief Marshall stepped in front of her. "Sorry, mam. Mr. Delamar is under arrest for the attempted murder of Mrs. Peedee Murray."

Dorothy uttered a swoon, and Steve stepped forward to steady her. Wilson's eyes suddenly registered awareness. He stared at Dorothy briefly, and then his eyes searched the room intently. His eyes fell on Margot. A rush of energy suddenly surged through him. With tremendous strength he wrested loose from the policemen and lunged for Margot. He was like a wild man, and Ben, Audrey, and Donald jumped in to help control him.

"You! I should have killed you when you were born! What a curse! What a curse to have a beautiful daughter like Annie-Ann die, and I'm left with this selfish, unappreciative little…" He threw his head back and began to wail, "She was beautiful, my little Annie-Ann. My sweet Annie-Ann. She would never let her daddy suffer like this. Making me grovel and beg. Beg like a pauper. No, Annie-Ann would do anything for her daddy. Anything. Why was *SHE* the one to die?" His head fell forward, then shot up again, hate emanating from his eyes. "You were supposed to find my note saying that the riptide warning was lifted. *You* were supposed to go out in the ocean. *You* were supposed to die not her. It's *your* fault she's dead."

Margot covered her mouth with her hand and recoiled in horror. Einer swept her into his arms and covered her ears with his hands.

219

"Get him out of here! Just get the dirty bastard out of my sight and out of my house," Einer said with fury in his voice.

The policemen pushed the struggling, obscene Wilson through the front door and to the waiting police car.

The Chief turned to Ben and said, "Sheriff, can you come down to the station and give us a statement about what went on here?"

"Sure, if you think you have room in your vehicle."

"We'll fit you in. Mr. Pellinger, we'll need statements from the rest of you, but it can wait until the storm passes."

"We'll be available, Chief. Thank you for your help and for coming out in this hurricane."

The Chief was delighted that Einer appreciated the effort of the James City County Police in arresting Wilson Delemar. He moved to the door and lifted his hat,

"Ladies." he said.

Dorothy was stunned by Wilson's outburst and by the revelation of why Annie-Ann drowned. Steve ushered her back into the library, and she slipped slowly into a chair.

She began to speak in a slow monotonous tone. "I stuck with him through so much. All the lies and pretense. All the embarrassing years of acting like we had money when there wasn't any. I stayed with him through all the women. I even stayed with him after he had that *disgusting* affair with that idiot girl whose father worked for the Pellingers. But just then, when he said he was responsible for the death of my lovely Annie-Ann, I wished he were dead."

Dorothy said nothing to acknowledge the hurtful things Wilson said about Margot.

"Dorothy, how did you get here?" Einer asked coldly.

"When the eye passed over I ran here. Wilson told me that he was coming to check on you, and that he might get stuck in the storm. I thought that's what had happened...that he was trapped here by the storm. Then when I saw how much devastation had occurred, I thought he'd been hurt or killed. Now I could kill him myself," Dorothy said.

Einer spoke efficiently and without sympathy. "We'll get you back as soon as possible."

"But..." Dorothy started to protest, then stopped.

"First we'll get you some dry clothes." Margot started to stand. "No, Margot. Not you. Have the maid help Dorothy find something to wear." Margot looked relieved. Dorothy looked miffed.

"I'll get Sara," Margot said.

"Ask Jack to come in, too," Einer added as he walked to the bar. It had been a long time between drinks, and he poured himself a big one. "Anyone else care for a drink?"

"I do," said Dorothy. Einer handed her a hefty portion of scotch. She took large swallows.

"I know a crisis is over is when I can sit down and have a drink," Einer rationalized as he sunk into his favorite chair.

Gradually the wind subsided, and the rain reduced to a steady drizzle. Could the hurricane finally be moving away from James City County? It seemed that as the threat of the storm vanished so did the threat to those at Berryhill.

Margot returned with Sara and Jack, the yardman. She avoided the hateful glare that Dorothy fixed on her. She crossed the room with aplomb and took a seat beside Einer. He reached out and touched her hand. A look of envy and disgust crossed Dorothy's face. She'd never experienced that kind of devotion.

"Sara, please help Mrs. Delamar find some dry clothes. And Jack, do you think you can get her home in the Jeep?" Einer said.

"No problem," replied Jack eagerly. He was excited to experience the challenge of driving the Jeep through the obstacles and mud left by the hurricane.

Chaper 25

"You just gotta see this Ignatius!" Matt exclaimed as he rushed into the library. His breath came in deep short pants, and he smelled of salty river water. His face was red from exertion, and his hair windblown.

At first Ignatius was startled, but he quickly relaxed when he realized Matt's outburst resulted from excitement, not alarm. "See what? Where you been?"

Matt began to push Ignatius' chair towards the door.

"Hey, let go. I do this myself," Ignatius demanded. "Where the hell are we going?"

"To the river. You just got to see this!" Matt repeated.

Ignatius abruptly clipped on the brakes to the wheelchair preventing Matt from taking matters into his own hands again. "Just how do you think I'm going to get through those woods and down to the river? You've lost your mind."

"No it's alright. There's a small road cut through the woods down to the river. It's used to get boats to the water," explained Matt.

"I'm going to wheel down some steep pig path to the river? I don't think so," protested Ignatius.

Matt laughed. "Lemme explain. Jack's going to drive us down in the Jeep. Come on. You've got to see this."

Matt's enthusiasm was contagious. "Well, this better be damned good. Risking life and limb. And for what?" Ignatius was already moving towards the front door.

Matt and Jack helped Ignatius into the Jeep and buckled him in. Then Jack drove the Jeep slowly down the steep, bumpy path avoiding as many potholes as possible, and stopped at the very edge of the James River. The sight was a wonder to behold. Three and four foot waves crashed in rapid succession onto the sandy river beach. Debris tossed upon the shore was quickly retrieved by the next wave and taken out again. Dead fish and crabs littered the bank, and waterfowl emerged from their shelter excited by the sight of such an abundance of food. The sounds and smells were invigorating to Matt. They were reminiscent of ocean surf.

Ignatius stared in awe. "I didn't know there were waves like this on a river."

"There isn't ordinarily. Or at least not like this," said Matt. "This is the result of the hurricane."

"You told me the hurricane was over," Ignatius said fearful that Matt had made some outrageous mistake.

"It is over," laughed Matt. "This is some kind of aftermath. It takes the river a while to settle down after so much wind and rain. Incredibly it looks just like ocean surf."

"Never having seen the ocean, I'll have to take your word for it. But regardless, it is spectacular," Ignatius said.

* * *

He closed the door to the interrogation room, and Ben accompanied Audrey and Donald into the Chief's office. The Chief poured them cups of thick, black coffee. They sat in silence blowing and sipping the scalding coffee and discussing the strange events of the past few days. The ringing of the phone interrupted their conversation.

The Chief lifted the receiver and said, "Yeah?" There was a long pause and he simply repeated, "Yeah." And hung up.

"We got ourselves a mess over on Jamestown Road. Dam broke and a lot of people can't get into their homes. Road's washed out, and a bridge is gone. We're using John Tyler as a detour. Of course, the folks out here are gonna love that." The Chief paused. "What a time for a murder investigation to reach climax…right in the middle of a hurricane."

"Chief," Ben said, "being from Tennessee, this is my first hurricane, and I hope my last. I never saw so much rain in all my life."

The Chief laughed. "We had a head start on the rain. This was more than we usually get, even in a hurricane." Changing the subject, the Chief returned to the business at hand. "Well, Sheriff, what do you think of our suspect?"

"He's some piece of work, Chief. Fortunately, I don't get too many murders out in Franklin County, Tennessee, but I'd have to say that I can't recall any case where a man fingered his family like that."

"Familial homicide," said Audrey.

Ben flashed the silly grin he'd been using every time Audrey spoke. "What do you mean familial homicide?" he asked.

"That's what you call murdering members of your own family…familial homicide," she explained and then looked down shyly, averting Ben gaze.

"I don't care what you call it," said the Chief, "but I sure am glad you all were up there at Berryhill. Murder is bad enough, but investigating the murders of a man like Pellinger and his family is a law enforcement officer's worst nightmare. Can you imagine the scrutiny and the press looking down your neck all the time?"

"Money seemed to be at the root of all of Delamar's schemes," said Audrey. "He started way back with Annie-Ann. Of course, he thought Margot would be the one to go in the ocean during the riptide alert. That's why Margot was heavily insured and Annie-Ann wasn't."

"Yeah, if there had been a big policy on Annie-Ann, her death would have raised a red flag," said Ben.

"How do you suppose Delamar knew the contents of Pellinger's will?" Donald wondered aloud. Being around good-natured Ben made him feel more confident.

"Oh, there's so many ways. People like Delamar make it their business to know other people's business. That's how they manage to live the way they do. He's cultivated sources for everything. Why he probably knows more about some families around here than their lawyers and priests do," said the Chief.

"And I'm sure he'd use that information if the need arose," said Audrey.

"Seems to me like Delamar is a smart enough fella that he could come up with a better scheme to get at the Pellinger money than killing three family members," Ben said shaking his head.

The Chief picked up a pencil from his desk and began to toy with it. Finally he spoke as if to himself. "According to Delamar, the bulk of the estate is willed to

Margot, of course. But Einer also provided generously for Noah and Mrs. Peedee. Nothing for Delamar or his wife."

"And that set Delamar off," interjected Audrey.

"Yeah, he let his greed get the best of him. He wanted it all to go to Margot," added Ben.

"But if Margot got it all, how would that benefit Delamar?" Donald was confused.

"Control, Donald," said Audrey. "Delamar thought he could control Margot again. He'd done it before when she was a girl. She'd been so easy then, but Delamar failed to recognize how she'd become more confident. That's probably why he went berserk when he asked Pellinger for more money and Margot didn't side with him. He realized he didn't have as much control over her as he thought."

"But if he killed Noah, Mrs. Peedee, and Einer, and he didn't have control over Margot, where would that get him?" asked Donald.

"Then he hoped that Margot would be arrested for killing her husband, her aunt, and her cousin. Delamar decided to commit the murders in the middle of the hurricane because there would be less chance of an interruption. He had already taken care of Noah, and he planned to kill Mrs. Peedee Murray and Mr. Einer Pellinger last night. It would appear that Margot was the only other person in the house at the time of the murders, and she would benefit from the deaths. So naturally she would be the number one suspect. Margot would be devastated, and unable to defend herself," the Chief explained.

"But how does that get him to Margot's inheritance?" Donald was still confused.

"Easy," said Audrey. "He was certain she'd crack following the deaths of three people she loved most. Then he'd encourage her to plead insanity, and who better than her father to take care of her estate while she's packed away in some institution or prison. But I got a question. Chief, you mentioned that Delamar chose the night of the hurricane because only Margot, Pellinger, and Ms. Peedee would be there. What about the hired help?"

"I checked that out," the Chief replied. "They have rooms in the kitchen wing that is far apart from the rest of the house. As a matter of fact, it's almost like being in another building. For all of Delamar's purposes, he thought the three family members were the only ones home."

"What about all the house guests?" asked Donald.

"On the day of Delamar's argument with Pellinger, Dorothy Delamar overheard Carrie tell Margot that she wanted to go back to Portsmouth immediately. So she told Delamar that Steve and Carrie left that day. She inadvertently told Delamar that his three intended victims were there alone," Ben explained.

"But what about you Sheriff, and your two friends?" Donald asked not wanting to leave a page unturned.

"When Old Wilson came a tearing out of Berryhill after that fuss with Einer, he was so riled up that he didn't recognize us in Ignatius' unfamiliar vehicle," Ben said shaking his head. "Poor old Wilson Delamar. He never reckoned on a bunch of company moving into Berryhill and upsetting his plans."

Tension and nights of interrupted sleep finally caught up with the exhausted policemen. They sat in silence, reflecting upon the interrogation that exposed Wilson Delamar's plot. Even Delamar's lawyer was shocked. He continuously cautioned his client to keep silent, but Wilson plunged ahead relentlessly as floodgates of guilt and remorse burst open.

The question had to be asked. Audrey said, "I don't understand Delamar's motive for writing that note naming Einer as Noah Murray's father. What purpose did that serve?"

The Chief answered, "We may never know the answer to that one, Kelly. We've got Delamar's statement, and that's all we need for this murder case. I say some things are best left alone...if you get my drift," he said sternly.

Surprisingly, Audrey did not argue. She simply said, "Gotcha, Chief."

Chapter 26

They gathered around a battery-operated radio in the library to hear the damage reports of Hurricane Jean. They listened silently and intently, stunned by the magnitude of the destruction caused not only by wind but most often by rain.

It was noted that the residents of the Williamsburg/James City area had barely recovered from an ice storm the previous winter when Jean hit. More than fifteen inches of rain fell in the area. Jamestown was hit hard. Jamestown Road was split in half, and traffic was rerouted onto Route Five, and the merchants along Jamestown Road were suffering. An entire lake was drained, and water and sewer lines broke. The Powhatan Creek crept into townhouses, and the smell of rotting furniture and carpet permeated the air.

Although the Outer Banks did not suffer the destruction that was feared, businesses and private properties along the Beach Road sustained heavy damage, and a few places were totally destroyed. Some cottages on the ocean side of Beach Road had been built too close to the water's edge, and paths had been cut through the sand dunes for easy access to the beach. These places were the first to go. In front of other cottages entire dunes had been leveled to provide an unobstructed view of the ocean. So without the dune protection, these ocean-side cottages were also destroyed or left tottering precariously over sinkholes while the angry sea still battered them. Inspectors quickly posted CONDEMNED signs on the doomed buildings.

Farther inland was a more distressing story. Parts of eastern North Carolina were devastated. Gentle streams and creeks raged angrily and poured over their banks flooding homes, farms, and businesses. Farm animals perished and some people were retrieved from their flooded homes in small fishing boats while others perched upon roofs and in trees awaiting their turn at rescue. The Governor continued to appeal for help from any source, and as volunteers arrived they were astounded by the magnitude of the destruction. Entire towns were not spared. Goldsboro, Rocky Mount and many other small cities watched in horror as parking lots turned into lakes, and merchandise floated in the muddy water that swamped their stores and businesses.

The hurricane had moved slowly northward to the small town of Franklin in southeastern Virginia. On Wednesday Hurricane Jean poured fifteen inches of rain on the already rain-soaked town. The Nottoway River had been carefully monitored, but no threat was feared from the Blackwater River. Ironically, as if nature were taunting the citizens, the water from the Blackwater River rose higher and higher until its banks could no longer hold it back. Water gushed into the downtown area engulfing more than one hundred eighty businesses and at least a hundred homes. The business section of Franklin ultimately laid under twenty inches of water.

Reports revealed that large cities fared no better. Newport News, Virginia, famous for its ship building industry, received seventeen inches of rain. Many hurricane evacuation routes were under water rendering them useless, yet miraculously no lives were lost. Red Cross volunteers and city work crews were already at work. Governors from

Virginia and North Carolina requested that their states be declared a disaster area.

The listeners sat transfixed as story after story of bravery, sacrifice, and compassion was recounted. Never having experienced a hurricane, Ignatius was especially moved. "How often do you have these damned hurricanes?" he asked.

"There's a hurricane season every year," explained Matt. "Runs roughly from August to October. There are several hurricanes per season. Of course, they're not all as destructive as Jean."

"Hurricane season? They got a season?" asked Ignatius.

Matt laughed. "The hurricane season is those months when weather conditions are most likely to generate hurricanes. The peak of the season is around September 10 of each year. But don't worry, with hurricanes you get a lot of warning. No one need lose his life in a hurricane. You have plenty of time to prepare or to evacuate."

"Well, I'm amazed that no one lost their life over in Newport News," Ignatius said.

"They took precautions," Einer stated simply. "Went to higher grounds, didn't go to work or school, stayed in and out of it...not like those damned fool weather reporters who go down on the beaches and dance around in the wind and rain trying to entertain their viewers."

"Einer's right," said Steve. "It takes days for these storms to cross the Atlantic and bump into the United States. People have plenty of warning. Of course, foolish kids have plenty of time to plan a hurricane party, too. Right, Matt?" He winked.

"Foolish is right," said Matt. "We were foolish."

Margot stood up, "Well, I don't want to hear any more right now," she said. "I've had enough. Carrie, let's go upstairs and think of something less stressful to talk about. Aunt Peedee, do you want to come?"

"I'll go upstairs, dear, but I think I'll go to my room," said Peedee

The three women left the room together. Matt, Ignatius, and Steve watched Einer as he walked toward the bar. He poured himself a large bourbon and returned to his favorite chair. He was seldom without a drink in his hand these days. The men sat silently each lost in his own thoughts. Ignatius reached for his pipe. Pete eyed his master and recognized the pipe preparation as a soothing ritual. He trotted across the room, and lay peacefully at Ignatius' side awaiting his usual ear scratch. Ignatius reached down and scratched his ear. Then he reached for the tobacco and filled the bowl to just the precise capacity. From his shirt pocket, he removed an ornate brass tamp, and tamped the tobacco firmly. Then striking a match, he lit the pipe in a single attempt. Soon he was enveloped in a cloud of smoke.

"I'm beginning to get used to the smell of pipe tobacco," said Einer. "I'll miss it when you're gone, Ignatius."

"Well, don't take up the habit," advised Ignatius.

From the coach road, the sound of an approaching car engine was heard. Pete, who was beginning to feel at home, ran to the front door to greet the newcomer. The slam of a car door was followed by quick footsteps on the porch. When the door opened, Pete raced back to report to Ignatius that Ben had returned from the police station.

"Well it's about time," grumbled Ignatius.

"You worried about me 'Natius?" Ben joshed. "Didn't know you cared."

"Huh!" scoffed Ignatius. "I got more important things to worry about than you."

The other men smiled at their friendly banter. "We're anxious to hear what went on at the police station," said Matt.

"Yeah, at first we were afraid they locked you up for getting involved in their investigation. Then we remembered that cute little police woman, and we knew she'd take care of you…any way she could," said Steve.

The men laughed. Ben's blushed.

Einer spoke bringing solemnity back into the conversation. He said hopefully, "Why don't you tell us what went on, Ben. That is if it won't compromise the case."

"Oh, it won't interfere with the investigation none. Old Wilson has laid the case out for them pretty well. Once he started talking, he was like a dam with a hole in it…everything came gushing out. His lawyer couldn't shut him up. By the way Einer, that was real decent of you to send his lawyer down there after all he tried to do to you and your family."

"Everyone is entitled to counsel," said Einer, "no matter how nefarious the deed. So tell us then."

Ben recounted the entire interrogation. He shared the police's suspicion that since Wilson's parents were heavily insured, perhaps they did not die accidentally. He told how Wilson insured Margot and schemed for her to go into the ocean during a heavy riptide warning. But Annie–Ann read his note which said all was clear and went to her death instead. Much to Einer's surprise, Ben told of Wilson's knowledge of the contents of Einer's will. Ben gave the details of how Delamar planned to kill Einer and his beneficiaries, Noah and Peedee. And Ben explained that since Margot was the only other family member in the house when Einer and Peedee were killed, naturally she'd be the suspect. And finally, he described how Wilson hoped to gain control of Margot's inheritance once she was in prison, institutionalized, or perhaps even executed.

They sat in silence. They were stunned at such maliciousness. The men sensed the hate Einer felt for Wilson. How could a father plot such evil for his own child? They wondered at the horror Einer must feel realizing that the love of his life had been in such jeopardy. For years he protected and loved her. Last night he almost lost her to the devil himself.--her own father.

Ben broke the silence. "And there is another thing I better mention, Einer," he said slipping to the edge of his chair and lowering his voice. "The note came up again. They raised the question about why Wilson wrote the note saying you were Noah's father. The Chief made a real strong point of telling Audrey…uh, Detective Kelly, to drop it. And I think they'll do just that. But I thought I'd better tell you. Things have a way of getting out. Margot could find out from someone else, you know."

"Thanks Ben," said Einer. "I'm not sure what to do about that."

Everyone stirred uncomfortably. Ignatius said, "Well the decision is yours, Einer, but you better think on it. This time it may be best to let sleeping dogs lie as we've said before."

"Perhaps this sleeping dog has lied too long," Einer said.

"I think I know why he wrote that note," said Ben.

"Well, let's hear it," Ignatius said restlessly.

"I think that he was setting up another motive for Margot to murder Einer," explained Ben.

Ignatius barked, "No point trying to analyze the criminal mind. You can't make sense out of someone who's crazy enough to do things like that to his family."

"Ignatius is right, you know. The man's evil in my opinion," said Matt. "Just plain evil, and he makes no sense."

"That's well and good, fellas, but the law don't work that way. They like things wrapped up real nice...no lose ends," said Ben. "I also think it could have been argued that Margot killed Miz Peedee and Noah because she didn't want to share Einer's estate with them."

"I see," said Steve. "Wilson wanted it to look like she killed Einer out of jealousy of the affair, and she killed Peedee and Noah so she wouldn't have to share Einer's estate. I believe we better rethink whether Wilson is crazy. Crazy like a fox, I say."

Ben was determined to pursue the question of the note. He said, "So, Einer, this brings me to the big question. You gonna take a chance that Margot never hears 'bout the affair with Mary and that you could be Noah's father, or are you gonna tell her yourself?"

The library door opened, and a strong, assured voice spoke, "Exactly what will you tell her, Einer?" Peedee stepped into the room and quietly closed the door behind her.

Chapter 27

The men stirred uncomfortably as Peedee slowly crossed the library and stood facing them. They wondered how much she heard and how much she understood of what she heard. The silence seems interminable. This could turn into a heated family altercation, and again the guests were faced with the decision to leave or stay.

Einer finally spoke, "Peedee, our conversation involved a part of the investigation that you are not privy to. Without all the information, you could not possibly understand..."

"Understand that you had an affair with Noah's mother? Understand that after she died you placed Noah in the loving care of the Birdsongs? Understand that you arranged for Will and me to adopt him? Understand that you always kept an eye on him, even when he was safely with us? Understand that you provided for him in your will? Is there anything left that I don't understand, Einer?" Peedee said calmly.

The men looked perplexed, and Peedee just stood there as if awaiting an answer to each of her questions. Her eyes were fixed on Einer, and he could not determine her feelings from her inexpressive stare.

His hand shook, and bourbon spilled as he lifted his glass. When he spoke, his voice lacked its usual confidence. He merely asked, "How did you know about this, Peedee?

"So *I* must answer questions first?" she asked rhetorically. She sighed, "I was standing in the hallway the night the officers came to question you about the note. Later I heard you tell these gentlemen about it. Now, Einer, please answer my questions. Don't you think I understand the circumstances?"

"I don't know. I simply don't know if you can understand," he said rubbing his eyes with the back of his hand.

Peedee went to Einer and dropped onto a stool facing him. She took his hand in hers and looked deeply into his eyes. "Einer Pellinger, of course I understand. Even though you were just a very young man, you handled things responsibly. You found a loving couple to take care of Noah, and they were even kind enough to allow his grandfather to visit. Then you told Will and me about Noah, and Einer, those were the happiest day of our lives. I understand. I think it is you who does not."

Relief swept over Einer's face. "Thank you Peedee. It means a great deal to me that you feel this way, but I'm not sure Margot would."

"Einer, you have been so wrapped up in your devotion to Margot and in protecting her, that you fail to realize how she has grown in confidence and understanding. Margot is stronger than you realize," Peedee said.

"Then you think she'll understand?" he asked.

"I think you should give her a chance to understand," Peedee answered.

"Huh," the ever-present voice of cynicism came from Ignatius. He said, "You know, it hasn't been determined that Einer is truly Noah's father. It seemed to me that Dorothy thought Wilson might be his father. Until that determination is made, seems best to leave it alone. Of course, there are DNA tests now to determine the father if you really want to be sure."

Peedee released Einer's hand and stood up, "Well," she said with conviction, "Einer can make that decision for himself, but I *know* who Noah's father was."

"Who?" asked Matt.

"Einer," Peedee answered confidently.

"How do you know?" asked Matt.

"Because Noah was so much like Einer. He had that strong sense of responsibility. In spite of his handicap, he took care of things...of sick and injured animals and birds. Like Einer, he was filled with compassion. Why his pity for trapped crabs is what got him into so much trouble the last few months of his life. Noah was kind and loving. And scoff if you will, Mr. Harder, I know Noah protected me from Wilson's assault. No, I don't need a DNA test to tell me who Noah's father is. Noah's father was not that evil Wilson Delamar. Noah's father is Einer."

Chapter 28

A cool breeze floated up from the James River and chilled the three men who stood on the front porch of Berryhill mansion. Gradually the early morning air warmed as a brilliant sunlight streamed through shattered leaves left dangling from the battered branches of giant oak trees. Hurricane Jean had breathed the last gasp of summer.

Ignatius, Steve, and Matt watched from the porch as a make shift, clean-up crew marshaled by Jack, the yard man, gathered rubble and tossed it into the beds of their pick-up trucks. The deafening sound of electric saws pervaded the grounds of the plantation as broken limbs and downed trees were cut into logs of suitable size for burning in Berryhill fireplaces. A construction contractor inspected for damage and made a list of needed repairs. Workers from the power company checked for hot electric wires and became the job of stringing the lines. Technicians checked the septic tank and pump house, and collected water samples for analysis.

Inside, Carrie and Peedee helped Lexie fill large pots of water to boil and use for cleaning. From the pantry, they brought jugs of bottled water for cooking and drinking until Berryhill's tap was determined safe.

Inside his library, Einer assembled homeowner's policies, telephone numbers of contact people, lists of damages, and a sheet on which to record expenses. Einer heard the clatter of glass and looked up as Margot crossed the room carrying a tray ladened with a small teapot, two cups and saucers, lemon, sugar, and cream. Einer was relieved to see that she looked more rested than he had seen her in several days.

She smiled and set the tray upon the desk. "Here, Einer, I thought you might like a cup of tea." She poured the steaming brew into a cup and without needing to inquire added just the right amount of lemon and sugar. She placed the cup in front of Einer and poured a second cup. To her cup she added sugar and cream. They sipped the tea silently, relishing the return of their favorite rituals. Although Wilson's crimes and arrest saddened Margot, she felt strangely liberated. It was as if the dastardly secrets that were laid bare empowered her and released her from any responsibility to the Delamars.

Einer smiled at his young wife and noted a touch of gray hair at her temples and a few fine lines around her mouth. He sensed her new strength and this prompted his decision. He said, "My dear, there is something I must tell you."

Margot suddenly looked apprehensive. "Einer is something wrong?"

Einer rose and walked around the desk. Taking her hands in his, he said, "No, just something that happened many years ago, and I'd like to share it with you."

He gently drew her up. "Let's go into the parlor, dear."

"Einer...?"

He steered her across the hall and into the parlor. Quietly, he closed the door behind them.

* * *

Matt, Steve, and Ignatius spotted Einer and Margot through the parlor window as Einer led Margot to the sofa and sat down beside her. The men quickly looked away and feigned interest in the grounds work.

"Looks like he made his decision," Steve said softly, eyes fixed on the workmen.

"Yes, I suppose he did," agreed Matt.

"Huh, well I hope he knows what the hell he's doing," grunted Ignatius.

The three men sat silently and focused intently on the activity in the yard, although their minds were on the discussion taking place in the parlor. After what seemed to be an interminable amount of time, they heard a door open and turned to see Margot and Einer walk onto the porch, arms around each other.

"Well, Matt, when do you think we oughta pull out of here," Ignatius said much relieved.

Matt smiled. "As soon as they open the Norfolk tunnel and clear Highway one sixty four to the beach."

Steve added, "Folks like to go to the beaches after a hurricane to see what's left…it anything. So it shouldn't be too long Ignatius before things open up. That tunnel's a main route for commuters. They'll have it open before you know it. Beach road, too. Of course, you can always go down and use the James River Bridge over to the south side. Now that's a little out of the way, but it'll get you there." Steve realized he was rambling.

Einer and Margot joined them, rapprochement on their faces. "What's this I hear?" asked Margot. "Don't tell me you're planning to leave?"

"Well, two of us are," said Ignatius nodding towards Matt. Then he added derisively. "I don't know about Ben. He's taken off with that policewoman, and Lord only knows where the hell they are."

Steve laughed. "Urbanna, Ignatius. Urbanna on the Rappahanock River. That's up in Middlesex."

"Well, with common names like those, I can't imagine why I didn't remember," Ignatius shot back peevishly.

"Audrey has a sailboat up at the marina, and she was going to show Ben the finer points of sailing," Matt explained.

"Finer points of sailing and whatever..." laughed Steve.

"Oh, Steve, you're awful." Margot chided her cousin and laughed.

"I'm surprised the Chief granted Audrey leave with things still in a mess from the hurricane," commented Einer. "Of course, I'm glad he did. She and Ben make a fine-looking couple."

"I think the Chief was so pleased with the way Audrey handled this case that he'd give her anything she asked," Matt said. "But Ignatius and I plan to go down to Nags Head as soon as we can. We'd like to try to salvage some of our vacation. We'll move on with or without our old buddy, Ben."

The five friends sat on the porch and watched the men at work on the grounds. Ignatius drew out his pipe, and on cue Pete scurried to his side and plopped down. Matt and Steve eyed the men's work critically and remarked to each other how they would do it differently...and better. And Einer and Margot held hands

243

and smiled. Berryhill Plantation had returned to its serene and elegant state.

* * *

Audrey's SUV sped east on highway thirty-three. Effects of the hurricane were apparent from the flooded fields and downed trees. She drove with one hand on the wheel while the other arm rested casually on the open window frame. Her thumb tapped the steering wheel in rhythm to the beach music playing on the radio. She wore her hair down, and it blew about freely. Suntanned arms reached out of the sleeveless, short tee shirt that exposed her taunt midriff, and her cut-off jeans accentuated the length of her tan legs. She wore no make-up and smelled of sunscreen lotion.

The burly figure seated on the passenger side could hardly keep his eyes off her as he squirmed uncomfortably in his new clothes. Audrey had taken Ben on a K-Mart shopping trip to purchase clothes for his first sailing trip. He'd bought stiff white athletic shoes to replace his comfortable, well-worn boots because she said that dark-sole shoes would scuff her boat. The new knit sweatshirt still smelled like K-Mart, and the scratchy denim shorts exposed his pale hairy legs. His aviator-styled sunglasses kept slipping down on his nose. He remembered how he'd stood in front of a tiny mirror and tried on countless pairs of sunglasses with the white price tags dangling from the nosepiece. Audrey had watched and laughed.

"What are you smiling about?" Audrey asked as she flipped the turn signal, and turned left onto highway two twenty seven.

"Just thinking about what a nice laugh you have. It's hearty, sincere...not one of those phony twittering laughs," Ben replied awkwardly. He was unaccustomed to paying compliments to women. His conversations with women were limited to the teasing he exchanged with his saucy, sassy secretary, Penny. He wondered how Audrey and Penny would get along. He shook his head and thought he'd never go there.

Audrey slowed down as they approached a bridge and a sign that read Urbanna. Half way across the bridge she stopped. "This is Urbanna Creek. The Rappahanock River is over there." She pointed. "This harbor is well protected. As you can see, you can't even tell a hurricane's been through."

"Looks like you chose a real safe spot, Audrey," said Ben. "I never seen so many sailboat masts sticking up in one place. 'Course we don't have many sailboats in Tennessee, so it don't take much to impress me."

"Sticks. We call them sticks," said Audrey.

Ben looked puzzled. She laughed, "Masts...we call the masts sticks. There's mine. Third boat from the right, this side of the dock. She's a twenty eight foot Hunter. Had her ten years and there's hardly a job on that boat I haven't tackled."

She drove the Jeep to the marina and parked it close to the clubhouse. They got a dock cart and filled it with enough supplies to last a week and 'to feed ten field hands' as Ben had said. Ben noticed that other boat owners greeted Audrey, and he received wide, knowing grins.

Ben pushed the cart brimming with supplies, and Audrey led the way to the boat. Ben was an adamant fisherman, so he boarded the sailboat sure-footedly. Audrey gave him the tour of the cockpit and the cabin complete with a well-equipped galley, head, and a v-berth stacked high with pillows and blankets. Ben eyed the V berth and wondered if his six foot two body could fit into that. "What the heck," he thought, "Sleep's not a priority."

After securing the supplies, Audrey fired the engine, and Ben threw off the lines. She backed the boat out of the slip with precision and turned the bow towards the creek.

"That was clean as a whistle, little lady," Ben said as he applied a lingering slap to her bottom.

She gave him a wary look. "Here, you take the wheel," she said. "Take her over there." She pointed towards the river.

Without hesitation, Ben grabbed the wheel and steered the boat in the direction Audrey pointed. As they moved to the mouth of the creek, Audrey explained the red and green river markers. She pointed to a gigantic, well-constructed osprey nest built on a river marker. Remarkably the nest survived the storm unscathed.

Soon they reached the mouth of the river and Audrey pointed to some crab pots. "There's probably not many out yet. The watermen haven't had a chance to get them in the water since the storm, but I'll still climb up on deck and point them out to you. Be real careful not to hit one. It can really mess up a propeller."

Ben was fascinated as he watched her scamper agilely onto the deck and begin pointing to the crab pots. He thought that they made a 'pretty good team'. Just when he thought he could not be more impressed, they came into the river. Audrey instructed him to point the boat into the wind and hold it there. She scurried about, and in no time flat, she'd raised the mainsail and unfurled the jib. Then cutting the engine, they were under sail.

"Audrey, you just impress the hell out of me," Ben said.

The ten mph winds made for a balmy, lazy sailing day. Audrey taught Ben different tacks and jibes, and she was delighted to discover he was not only at home on the water, but was also a quick learner. They ate sandwiches, drank soft drinks, and talked about everything except the Delamar case.

As the daylight began to wane, they sailed west to the Corrottoman River and brought down the sails. Firing the engine, they motored into the west branch cautiously picking their way through debris left by the hurricane. They anchored beside a ferry boat route. Then popping a couple of cans of beer, they settled in and leisurely listened to beach music and watched the cable boat ferry cars back and forth across the river. Daylight faded, and an osprey bleeped his return home. His enormous wings silhouetted the rosy sky as he circled the nest and landed softly beside his mate. Night sounds permeated the woods, and a cool breeze stirred the underbrush on the riverbank.

Audrey shivered. "Do you dance?" she asked.

"Who me? No mam. Never did learn to dance. When I was in school, I was too busy playing football to learn to dance."

Audrey took his hands and gave him a tug. He stood awkwardly. "You have to learn to dance, Ben," she teased. "Part of the sailing experience is cockpit dancing."

"Cockpit dancing?"

She put her arms around his waist and began to move slowly. "There's nothing to it. Since there's not much room in the cockpit, you just sorta move like this."

He locked his arms around her, and they swayed slowly back and forth in rhythm to old songs that revived memories of simpler times. Thoughts of the drudgery and intensity of their jobs were soon forgotten. A round moon bounced from the horizon casting golden ripples on the water. The boat rocked gently in cadence with their movements. Ben bent and softly kissed Audrey's neck. Then they stood perfectly still searching each others' eyes questioningly. Slowly they disappeared into the cabin, and the boat began to gently rock again.

Chapter 29

The green Jaguar turned right onto Route Five. The turn seemed automatic with no need to reference a map. The damage done by the recent hurricane was apparent, but did not diminish the driver's memory of this place. Her blonde hair sowed with gray flecks shined in the sunlight, and her pale green sweater set was accented with a jade scarf that matched her eyes precisely. She popped in a tape and a group began to sing, "Those were the days my friend, we thought they'd never end..." She smiled and began to sing along never missing a word. Flipping the right turn signal, she turned onto the coach road leading into Berryhill Plantation. Soon the road led onto a pebble driveway that ended at the steps to the mansion. She couldn't resist tapping the horn several times before bounding up the steps. She rang the bell and before the carillon was complete, Margot threw open the door.

She spread her arms and squealed, "Caryn! How wonderful to see you! You just missed Matt."

* * *

Gray plumes drifted above the pink cumulus clouds spanning the horizon. The wind blew from the ocean to the shore creating large, strong waves. Their thunderous sound produced an awesome, daunting effect as they crashed upon the sandy beach retrieving carelessly placed objects from the shore and taking them out to sea. It was low tide and conditions were perfect for surf kayaking.

Ignatius sat on the second-floor balcony of the condominium drinking a cup of his special blend coffee. He found the vastness of the ocean and endless expanse of the beach mesmerizing He watched as Matt crossed the sand, his rounded-bottom kayak held aloft. He wore a wet suit, helmet, life jacket and beach shoes.

Matt waited for a wave large enough to support his boat and faced his kayak straight into it. When a high wave rolled in he paddled hard and leaned into it in a ready-to-roll position. To avoid being broached, he continued to paddle straight into the waves. As wave after wave passed, he paddled hard maintaining a good speed to avoid moving backwards.

Finally he was beyond the breakers and was riding the swells. Now Matt relaxed and used short, quick strokes. The rising and falling of the waves beneath him was calming, almost hypnotic. He spotted Ignatius on the second-floor deck, but did not chance to wave for fear of losing his paddle. How he wished his friend could join him.

Surf paddling was exhausting, and Matt was definitely out of shape. It wasn't long before fatigue set in, and he headed wearily for shore. As he paddled in, he stayed between sets of waves. Finally he reached the breakers. In order to avoid being clobbered he waited for a good wave that was the last one of a set. Then he paddled behind it as closely as possible until he reached shallow water. Finally he hopped out on the ocean side of the boat, grabbed the boat, and dragged it ashore.

He trudged up the sand dune and secured his kayak under the building. Since he was exhausted, he chose the elevator instead of the steps. He punched the level two button and braced himself as his water legs quivered giving him the sensation of still being on the ocean.

When the elevator door opened, he found Ignatius stretched on a chaise lounge. He shared an afghan with Pete who shivered every time a seagull squawked and flew too close to the deck.

"He thinks it's a damned flying dog," explained Ignatius as he patted Pete reassuringly.

Matt gave Ignatius a hardy greeting. "Great ride, Ignatius. Perfect water for paddling."

"Looked like you had no problems. I see a lot of surfers out today, too."

"Yeah, the best waves for surfing are right after a big storm, and Jean certainly qualified as a *big* one."

Matt disappeared through the sliding glass door and returned wearing dry clothes and holding a cup of Ignatius' coffee. Matt inhaled the aroma of the dark liquid deeply and cupped his hands around the mug. Ignatius stared intently at the ocean.

"Well, what do you think?" asked Matt pulling up a rocking chair and joining him.

Ignatius inhaled the saltwater air deeply and sighed. "Matt, this is the most magnificent sight I've ever seen. When I left the southwest, I thought I'd never see anything to compare with the desert. But the ocean is similar to the dessert in so many ways...the vastness, the wild unpredictability, the human vulnerability. Even the noise is similar. Oh, I know you don't hear the crash of waves on the desert, but both places have sounds that are haunting, beckoning. Both possess a stirring, melancholy ambience."

Matt smiled and laid his head against the back of the rocker. He had never heard his friend speak so poetically.

"I'm sorry that the beach part of our vacation was cut short by Noah's death and Hurricane Jean. We could have spent more time down here," Matt said.

"Now I've told you," Ignatius said emphatically, "Stop fretting over two things that you can't control...death and the weather. Keep that up and you'll worry yourself into an early grave." Ignatius's customary surly attitude had returned.

Matt closed his eyes and listened as the screech of the gulls blended with the music that floated up from the beach through a cheap portable radio. He smiled and breathed deeply inhaling the brackish ocean air. He basked in the hot, autumn sunlight and delighted in the cool breeze that soothed his smarting skin. He welcomed the image that played on his eyelids...the image of a lovely porcelain face set with jade eyes that peered into his very soul. Her lips moved, but emitted no sound. The face bent to kiss him spilling sun-streaked hair across his chest, and she laughed. Her laughter mingled with laughter from the beach. Then the image began to slowly fade. No! Matt struggled to retain it. How many times he had dreamed of her, and every time the vision slipped away leaving him feeling empty, alone. The disappointment was always depressing. This was her place. Their place.

"Caryn!" Matt murmured as the image slowly faded until it completely vanished.

"Hey, Matt," said Ignatius, concern in his voice. He reached over and shook his arm. "Matt, you okay?"

252

Matt catapulted from his dream and wiped the sweat from his brow. "Yeah, I'm okay, Ignatius. Guess it's hotter than I thought."

"I heard what you said, Matt," Ignatius said plainly. "You called 'Caryn'. You get in touch with her before we left Williamsburg?"

"No"

"Why?"

"I don't know, Ignatius. I suppose I had other things on my mind," Matt said caustically.

Ignatius would not be put off. "Let me tell you something, Matt. You got a wound, and it's festering. If you don't tend to it, you'll never recover. Now that's all I'm gonna say about Caryn."

Matt shot back angrily, "Good. Cause you're beginning to sound like Ben." Then fearing he had offended his well-meaning friend, he added contritely, "I suppose I could get in touch with her."

"When?"

"Soon...maybe real soon."

"What are you afraid of?"

"Damn it, Ignatius, I'm afraid that when we finish sifting through all the "good old memories", there'll be nothing there."

Ignatius simply grunted and nodded his head.

Turning away from Ignatius, Matt closed his eyes. He breathed deeply and attempted to resurrect the images of Caryn. But with each breath, he became more frustrated. This was HIS dream. Why couldn't he recreate it? But like so many times before the fantasy evaded him. He heard the laughter of the swimmers as they raced up to the beach wet and cold and exhilarated. Matt heard the sound of car doors slamming as couples packed up their cars for the trip back home. He heard the whir of departing tires on the Beach Road. He could sense the disappointment in the squawk of the gulls as they realized that their benefactors were gone and so were the handouts. He felt the breeze as it turned cool and brisk. He recalled twilight walks along the beach with young friends who shoved and splashed and laughed at long forgotten absurdities.

One laugh stood out from the others. It was unfettered, vibrant, and yet gentle. The laugh was so real. If he could resurrect the sound, why couldn't he resurrect the image? He tossed his head fitfully.

"Caryn. Caryn," he whispered hoarsely.

"Matt."

The dream…maybe it's back. He turned in the direction of the voice and slowly opened his eyes. The fading sunlight created a soft aura about her gold and silver hair. It is back. The dream is back.

"Caryn," Matt repeated again softly. "I wish it were really you."

"And who else would it be, Matt?" she murmured.

Matt's eyes opened wide. "It is you. It really is. I can't believe it. You are here. What…How?"

"Well, Matt, one of us had to make the first move. We haven't another twenty-five years to wait. Now do we?" With eyes closed and lips parted, the porcelain face moved slowly towards Matt. He didn't answer. As Ignatius would say… *The question's rhetorical Matt.*"

THE END

CPSIA information can be obtained at www.ICGtesting.com
Printed in the USA
LVOW091819180712

290619LV00015B/65/P

9 781456 349813